Deannie couldn't go through with it.

Tears slipped down her cheek and pooled on the collar of her Western-cut wedding gown. Twisting Brodie Trueblood's engagement ring on her finger, Deannie fought off the oppressive guilt clutching her heart.

Marriage didn't scare her. Deceiving Brodie did.

Brodie deserved so much better.

She could already hear the wedding march. Deannie pictured the gaily decorated living room with all their friends gathered, waiting to witness her union with Brodie Trueblood.

Closing her eyes, she envisioned Brodie standing before the makeshift altar, his brown eyes shining with radiant love. A love that would be destroyed the minute he learned the truth about her.

Deannie moaned at the image. Better to leave him at the altar than marry him and live a lie.

Deannie had only one option—to get out of town as fast as possible.

Dear Reader,

This month, Silhouette Romance unveils our newest promotion, VIRGIN BRIDES. This series, which celebrates first love, will feature original titles by some of Romance's best-loved stars, starting with perennial favorite Diana Palmer. In *The Princess Bride*, a feisty debutante sets her marriage sights on a hard-bitten, cynical cowboy. At first King Marshall resists, but when he realizes he may lose this innocent beauty—forever—he finds himself doing the unthinkable: proposing.

Stranded together in a secluded cabin, single mom and marked woman Madison Delaney finds comfort—and love—in *In Care of the Sheriff*, this month's FABULOUS FATHERS title, as well as the first book of Susan Meier's new miniseries, TEXAS FAMILY TIES. Donna Clayton's miniseries MOTHER & CHILD also debuts with *The Stand-by Significant Other*. A workaholic businesswoman accepts her teenage daughter's challenge to "get a life," but she quickly discovers that safe—but irresistibly sexy—suitor Ryan Shane is playing havoc with her heart.

In Laura Anthony's compelling new title, *Bride of a Texas Trueblood*, Deannie Hollis would do *anything* to win back her family homestead—even marry the son of her enemy. In Elizabeth Harbison's sassy story, *Two Brothers and a Bride*, diner waitress Joleen Wheeler finds herself falling for the black-sheep brother of her soon-to-be fiancé…. Finally, Martha Shields tells a heartwarming tale about a woman's quest for a haven and the strong, silent rancher who shows her that *Home is Where Hank is*.

In April and May, look for VIRGIN BRIDES titles by Elizabeth August and Annette Broadrick. And enjoy each and every emotional, heartwarming story to be found in a Silhouette Romance.

Regards,

Joan Marlow Golan

Joan Marlow Golan
Senior Editor Silhouette Books

Please address questions and book requests to:
Silhouette Reader Service
U.S.: 3010 Walden Ave., P.O. Box 1325, Buffalo, NY 14269
Canadian: P.O. Box 609, Fort Erie, Ont. L2A 5X3

BRIDE OF A TEXAS TRUEBLOOD

Laura Anthony

Silhouette

R O M A N C E™

Published by Silhouette Books

America's Publisher of Contemporary Romance

To my two editors,
Melissa Jeglinski and Melissa Senate.
Thanks so much for your faith in me.

 SILHOUETTE BOOKS

ISBN 0-373-19285-1

BRIDE OF A TEXAS TRUEBLOOD

Copyright © 1998 by Laurie Blalock

This edition published by arrangement with Harlequin Books S.A.

Printed in U.S.A.

Books by Laura Anthony

Silhouette Romance

Raleigh and the Rancher #1092
Second Chance Family #1119
Undercover Honeymoon #1166
Look-Alike Bride #1220
Baby Business #1240
The Stranger's Surprise #1260
Bride of a Texas Trueblood #1285

LAURA ANTHONY

started writing at age eight. She credits her father, Fred Blalock, as the guiding force behind her career. Although a registered nurse, Laura has achieved a life-long dream and now pursues writing fiction full time. Her hobbies include jogging, boating, traveling and reading voraciously.

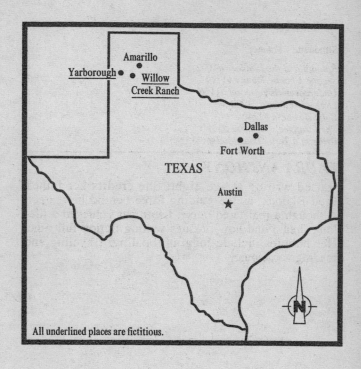

All underlined places are fictitious.

Prologue

She couldn't go through with it.

Deannie Hollis sat on the antique four-poster bed in the south bedroom of the rambling ranch house that until fifteen years ago had belonged to the Hollis family for four generations. She had even been conceived in this very bedroom. Now all she had to do to reclaim her birthright was to walk down the aisle and say ''I do'' to Brodie Trueblood.

It was that simple and that complicated.

Tears slipped down her cheeks and pooled on the white lace collar of her Western-cut wedding gown. A bouquet of white roses and baby's breath rested in her trembling hands and a salty lump burned her throat. Twisting Brodie's engagement ring on her finger, Deannie shook her head, trying her best to fight the oppressive guilt clutching her heart. The action set her pearl cluster earrings dancing below her earlobes and her mesh bridal veil brushing lightly against her shoulders.

She could not do this. Brodie deserved so much better. Sniffling, she reached for a tissue.

A knock sounded at the door.

"C-c-come in." Deannie hiccoughed and smoothed her white satin skirt with one hand.

Her sister-in-law to be, Patsy Ann Trueblood, poked her head in the door. "Preacher's here. Everyone's waiting."

"Could you give me ten more minutes?" Deannie asked.

Patsy Ann swished into the room in a lavender whirl and shut the door behind her. "Cold feet?" she asked, plopping down beside Deannie on the bed.

Deannie nodded.

"Oh, honey, you know you're getting the best man in all of Deaf Smith County."

"I know." *That* was the problem.

Patsy Ann patted her hand. "It'll be all right, I promise. If you love Brodie, and he loves you, nothing else matters."

But Patsy Ann was wrong. Dead wrong. She knew nothing of Deannie's dark secret.

"I know my marriage to Kenny isn't perfect," Patsy Ann chattered, "but we're working things out. And believe it or not, after seven years, our life together is better than it's ever been."

Deannie knew. She'd witnessed Kenny's transformation first-hand. "I'm glad you guys are happy," she said.

"We owe it all to you and Brodie. If it weren't for you two, Kenny and I would still be separated."

"Naw, Kenny's a good man. He would have come to his senses eventually."

Patsy Ann leaned over and gave Deannie a hug. "Come on, kiddo, don't let marriage scare you. It really is worth the effort."

Marriage didn't scare her. Deceiving Brodie Trueblood did.

"I need five more minutes alone," Deannie pleaded. "Please, Patsy Ann."

"Okay." Looking puzzled, her matron of honor left the room.

Deannie tried to take a deep breath and found she couldn't. Anxiety constricted her airway. A claustrophobic sensation gripped her stomach. She had to get out of here. Leave. Flee. Run. Now. Today. This very minute. Before it was too late.

Springing to her feet, she dashed to the window and pushed back the curtain. Brodie's pickup sat around back, already desecrated by well-wishers. White shoe polish proclaiming Just Married marred the windows, and dozens of tin cans hung from the bumper. Even if she had access to the keys, cars were parked around the circular driveway, blocking any exit.

She was stuck, stranded. What to do? She couldn't face Brodie, couldn't call off the wedding while looking him in the eyes. She was too big a coward for that.

Damn. She could hear strains of the wedding march coming from the living room.

In her mind, she saw the gaily decorated living room— vases of roses, white crepe paper streamers, satin doves, silk bows. She knew little Buster was there, clutching a pillow with their wedding rings pinned to it. And so was sweet Angel, dressed in ruffles and lace, carrying a basketful of white rose petals. She saw their friends, dressed in their best finery, gathered in the living room, waiting to witness the union of Brodie Trueblood and Deannie McCellan.

Only she wasn't Deannie McCellan as everyone believed.

Closing her eyes, she envisioned Brodie standing before the makeshift altar, his dark hair combed off his forehead, his brown eyes shining with radiant love. A love that would be destroyed the minute he learned the truth about her.

Deannie moaned at the vivid image. Agony, unlike anything she'd ever experienced, writhed through her. Better to leave him at the altar than marry him and live a lie.

She had tried to convince herself that love would be

enough. Self-denial had led her this far, but her conscience would not allow her to go any further with this charade. True love was based on honesty. How could she build a life with Brodie if she couldn't tell him the truth? No. Deannie had only one option and that was to get out of town as fast as possible.

But how to escape without detection?

Peering out the window again, Deannie searched the grounds below, desperate for a solution. She spotted Brodie's horse, Ranger, saddled in the paddock. Yes. That was it. She would take Ranger and clear out. Once she got to Yarborough, she would figure out where to go from there.

Her decision made, Deannie moved aside the sash and raised the window. With both hands she pushed out the screen. Hiking her dress around her waist, she placed a booted foot on the sill. One look at those white boots and her heart lurched in her throat.

Just two weeks ago she and Brodie had gone to the mall in Amarillo, and he'd picked out those boots especially for their wedding, claiming they would be perfect for his cowgirl bride.

Don't think about it, she admonished herself. Just go.

She hesitated a moment, calculating the distance to the ground from the second story. Taking a deep breath, she gathered her skirt in her hands.

"Here goes," she whispered and jumped.

Deannie landed feet first and stumbled backward from the impact. Recovering, she ran across the yard toward the paddock, flung open the gate and clicked her tongue at Ranger.

Obediently, the horse came to her. Pulse thudding like a snare drum, Deannie swung into the saddle.

The cool September breeze ruffled her hair as she grabbed the reins and aimed Ranger west toward the setting sun. Clouds bunched on the horizon, threatening rain.

Any minute now they would discover her gone. Any

LAURA ANTHONY 11

minute the atmosphere would change from festive to gloomy. Any minute Brodie Trueblood's heart would be broken, shattered just as surely as her own, their hopes and dreams crushed like rose petals beneath angry boot heels. Oh! why had she allowed herself to fall in love with him?

Regret, heavy and unshakable, filled her. Blinking back more tears, Deannie galloped away across the prairie. Her veil streaming out behind her, her train whipping against the saddle. Her hands, encased in soft white gloves, clutched the reins in a death grip.

Try as she might, Deannie couldn't stop her mind from being jettisoned back to that fateful day four months ago. The day she had returned to Yarborough, Texas, hell-bent upon revenge.

Chapter One

Four months earlier

"I'm looking for Rafe Trueblood," Deannie Hollis said to the man behind the bar.

She swept her gaze through the dimly lit honky-tonk. Even at four o'clock on a Monday afternoon the Lonesome Dove was crowded. A sad commentary on the rough economic times in Deaf Smith County. Too many people out of work. Too many people spending their unemployment checks drowning their sorrows in whiskey and beer. Too many people looking for love in all the wrong places.

"Well, sugar, I'm afraid you're about two weeks too late," the bartender drawled, leaning on the counter with both elbows.

"What do you mean?" Deannie asked, raising her voice to be heard above the jukebox where Hank Williams, Jr., was singing about family traditions.

"Haven't you heard?"

"Heard what?"

"Rafe Trueblood's dead."

Deannie stared at the bartender in stunned disbelief. It couldn't be true. Rafe dead? No! Not after she'd spent the past fifteen years plotting and planning her revenge against the man who'd cheated her father out of his house—his home and his inheritance. She had counted the years, months, weeks, days, hours, until she was old enough, wily enough and accomplished enough at poker to challenge that thieving varmint, Rafe Trueblood, to a card game and win back the family ranch the same way her daddy had lost it.

"Yep. Keeled over during a poker game. I, for one, will sorely miss the man. Rafe spent a good two hundred dollars a week in here. He was a big tipper, too."

Deannie sucked in her breath. Her whole body started trembling. The smell of stale cigarettes hung in the air, choking her. The noise from the jukebox echoed in her ears. A dry, bitter taste glutted her mouth. Blinking, she clutched the bar with both hands.

"Sugar?" The bartender's burly face blurred before her. "Are you all right?"

Her mouth opened but no words came out.

The bartender hurried around the bar and gently pushed her down onto a stool. "Rafe a good friend of yours, was he?"

"I didn't expect this," she said, lifting a hand to her throat.

"Well fifty-five years of hard, fast living finally caught up with old Rafe."

Staring at the scarred linoleum floor, Deannie tried to come to grips with the news. What was she going to do now? It appeared that her life's goal of reclaiming the family homestead had died along with the gambler.

"Rafe's son, Kenny, is in the back room," the bartender said, squatting down in front of her. "I don't normally let strangers go back there because sometimes the boys indulge in a little illegal gambling, but seein' as how you were a friend of Rafe's..."

"Thank you," Deannie whispered. She'd forgotten Rafe Trueblood had two sons. After all, she'd only been seven when she and her daddy had been forced to leave their home at Willow Creek Ranch and move into a squalid one-bedroom apartment in Amarillo.

From what the bartender said, Kenny Trueblood must have followed in his father's disreputable footsteps. Pensively Deannie considered her next move. Why did she have to change her plans? She could win Willow Creek Ranch back from Kenny just as easily as she could have won it from Rafe. Maybe even easier.

"Come on." The bartender took her by the hand and led her past a string of curious customers eyeing them from the bar.

They pushed through two sets of double doors and into a storeroom dominated with fat-bellied men and a poker table. Six pairs of eyes swung to take in Deannie.

"Kenny," the bartender said, gesturing to the youngest, most attractive man in the room. "This little gal came in looking for your daddy."

A huge smile rippled across Kenny Trueblood's face as his gaze raked the length of Deannie's body. His crude once-over left her feeling unclothed. Crossing her arms over her chest, she met his stare with a frown.

"You're a little young," Kenny assessed, "even for the old man's eclectic tastes."

"I wasn't his girlfriend," Deannie replied. She wasn't unnerved by the intense scrutiny that greeted her. This wasn't the first time she'd been the recipient of male admiration. She'd spent her fair share of time in honky-tonks following after her father, and she could take care of herself.

"I gotta get back to work," the bartender said, jerking his thumb toward the bar. "You fellas play nice."

"We're always nice," one man grumbled and swallowed a long swig from his beer bottle. That comment generated a collective chuckle from the men assembled.

Deannie lifted her chin and tried her best to look tough. This was it. The moment she'd been waiting for, although the showdown was somewhat anticlimactic after the news of Rafe's death.

"How come you were asking after my daddy?" Kenny questioned, dusting off an empty chair and patting the seat. Tentatively Deannie inched over and sat down next to Kenny. He smelled of beer and peanuts and aftershave.

"I came to play cards," she declared. "I heard if you want to test your skills at five-card stud, Rafe Trueblood is the man to beat."

One fellow hooted. "Are you serious?"

The guy sitting on Deannie's right choked on his beer and sputtered. His friend pounded him on the back.

"What's this?" The bearded giant shuffling cards demanded. "The kid thinks she could have beaten the likes of Rafe?"

Kenny held up a hand and tried hard to disguise his knowing smirk. "Come on, Lou, give the lady a chance."

"You saying we should deal her in?" Lou looked incredulous.

"Got something against taking money from children?" Kenny asked.

"I'm no child," Deannie insisted, thrusting out her jaw. "I'm twenty-two years old."

"All right." Lou dealt the cards. "Seven-card draw, nothing wild. If you're dumb enough to play, ante up, girly. Ten-dollar minimum."

Deannie pushed a lock of hair from her forehead. "I'll need some chips."

"Here you go, sugar," one man said, presenting her with a rack of poker chips.

"What's your name?" Kenny asked, leaning closer and striking a match against his thumbnail to light a cigar.

The action, so much like his father's, sent a shudder through her memory. "Deannie McCellan," she said, using her mother's maiden name. She had not planned on revealing her true identity until she'd won back her ranch from the Truebloods.

"Where are you from, Deannie?"

"Amarillo."

"Where'd you hear about Rafe?"

Deannie shrugged. "Here and there."

"You can do better than that." Kenny arched an eyebrow and casually draped one arm across the back of her chair.

Deannie took a deep breath. "My father used to play cards with a man named Gil Hollis. From what I understand, Rafe was such a good card player he won Mr. Hollis's ranch in a poker game. Is that correct?" Struggling to maintain her best poker face, she met Kenny's eyes with a challenging stare.

Looking uncomfortable, Kenny gnawed on the end of his cigar. "Yeah," he said. "It's true."

"Your father must have been some gambler, Mr. Trueblood. Did you know Gil Hollis got so depressed, he eventually committed suicide over the shame of losing his family homestead? He never recovered from the humiliation."

Kenny cleared his throat and dropped his gaze. "No. I wasn't aware of that. Sorry to hear about it. But a bet's a bet. Wasn't Rafe's fault that Hollis guy had such a weak character."

Deannie bit down hard on her bottom lip to contain the sudden spurt of anger shooting through her at Kenny's callous words. The man was speaking about her daddy! How she longed to tell him exactly what she thought about him and all the low-life Truebloods.

"We gonna play cards or we gonna chat?" Lou grunted.

Just then the door creaked open. Raising her head, Deannie looked up to see a tall, lean cowboy silhouetted in the light from the bar.

He walked with an easy, self-confident stride. His mouth was set in hard, firm lines and his brown eyes glanced harshly around the table. Settling his hands on his low-slung hips, he stared at Deannie, then shifted his gaze to Kenny and back again. The expression flitting across his face told Deannie he'd made an erroneous assumption about her relationship with Kenny Trueblood.

"Dammit, Kenny," the man exploded, his voice booming in the room's small confines. "What in the hell are you up to?"

"Don't get your underwear in a knot, little brother, it's not what you think."

"Hey, Brodie, pull up a chair," Lou invited.

"I got better things to do than get drunk and lose money at cards," Brodie Trueblood said before turning his attention back to his brother. "For your information, Kenny, while you're sitting here playing footsie with some underage bar dolly, your wife's in labor with your third child. Thought you might like to know."

Brodie Trueblood was a sight to behold. He held his head high, his shoulders straight. He was a man of principle. Deannie could read his character in his stance, his posture, the way he chose his words. Brodie's nostrils flared and his bottom lip curled in disgust.

Watching him had Deannie's heart racing. He gave the appearance of tightly contained dynamite. He would never explode unprovoked but heaven help the creature who deserved this man's wrath.

Kenny stood, his chair scraping loudly across the cement floor. "Hey! Don't get high-and-mighty with me. You aren't married—you have no idea what it's like. Patsy Ann and I are separated. She's the one who left me, remember?"

"I wonder why," Brodie said coldly, then turned on his heels and stalked out the door.

The room fell silent. Nobody looked at Kenny.

"Guess you'll be wantin' me to deal you out, huh?" Lou said.

"What the hell for?" Kenny asked, angrily knocking back the rest of his beer.

"You're not going to the hospital?" Deannie asked, not shocked by Kenny's cavalier behavior. He was, after all, Rafe Trueblood's son.

"Aw." Kenny waved a hand. "Patsy Ann labors for a good ten hours, and Brodie overreacts. I got lots of time. Ante up, everyone."

Sometimes Brodie Trueblood wanted to take his older brother by the front of the shirt and shake him silly. Unfortunately, Kenny had inherited their father's disreputable tendencies, drinking and gambling chief among them. Now it seemed Kenny had added womanizing to the list.

Gritting his teeth, Brodie blasted from the parking lot. Who was the foxy young redhead that had been sitting next to Kenny? Brodie didn't recognize her and he knew almost everyone in Yarborough.

That skimpy little outfit she'd been wearing spoke volumes. The emerald green color set off her fiery hair, and the silky material had slid across her skin like rippling water. Though he'd tried not to notice, the deep, plunging vee neckline had announced to the world she was darn proud of her cleavage and rightfully so.

He had to admit Kenny's good taste. The woman was a beauty. Even in the dim bar lighting, her well-sculpted features were evident, from her high cheekbones to her slender, aristocratic nose, and she was far classier than the typical barroom groupie.

Question was, what in the hell was she doing with Kenny? Finding out his brother had a third child on the way would probably put a crimp in her affections, Brodie thought wryly, and turned his pickup truck in the direction of Deaf Smith County Hospital. Somebody ought to be there with Patsy Ann, since his brother wasn't man enough to own up to his responsibilities. Sometimes the thankless chore of single-handedly redeeming the Trueblood name was a job Brodie longed to relinquish.

Why did Kenny treat his wife so cruelly? Brodie speculated. Couldn't he see the pain he was causing the mother of his children? Shame for his brother's actions burned Brodie's craw. He hoped like hell Patsy Ann never found out about that redhead.

Again Brodie wondered about the stranger. There was something provocative about her. The tilt of her head, maybe, or the gleam in her icy blue eyes. No matter. He knew the type—sexy as hell but interested in only one thing—money. Yep. That redhead spelled nothing but trouble. Hadn't Daddy dallied with a long string of such women? They'd brought him only grief.

Brodie winced. He hated remembering the bad things his daddy had done to his mama. Cheating on her, gambling away the grocery money, disappearing for days at a time, then turning up drunk as a skunk. Or else they would get a call from one jailhouse or the other, wanting Mama to come post the old man's bail.

The only thing worthwhile Rafe Trueblood had ever done was to win Willow Creek Ranch and even that was an ill-gotten gain.

But despite the underhanded way his father had obtained the property, Brodie loved Willow Creek with all his heart. The place meant something to him. It was home. Until Rafe had managed to cheat the ranch away from Gil Hollis, the Truebloods had lived a roller-coaster life. Moving from one flophouse to the next, flying high when Daddy hit it big in a poker game, subsisting on rice and beans for weeks at a time when he lost money on the ponies.

Then Rafe had lucked out and buffaloed poor Gil Hollis into betting his entire inheritance on one hand of cards.

At last his mother had had a home of her own. He and Kenny had been able to finish high school in Yarborough. For the first time in his life, they'd lived in one place long enough to make friends. Although it had been tough in the beginning. Not too many of the townsfolk were happy to hear that one of their own had been swindled by an itinerant gambler like Rafe Trueblood.

Brodie had tried to justify his father. Losing the ranch was Gil Hollis's own fault, he'd rationalized. The man should never have gambled away something as precious as Willow Creek. Then he'd discovered that Gil Hollis had started drinking and gambling only after his wife's tragic death in a riding accident.

Braking for a stoplight at the corner of Ninth and Gardenia, Brodie remembered the day he'd gone to his father and asked him to give the ranch back to Mr. Hollis and his daughter. Dang if he could recall that little girl's name. Rafe had laughed in his face and called him a "bleeding-heart pansy." Brodie frowned at the distasteful memory. Dear old Dad. Quite the sentimentalist.

Unable to help Mr. Hollis, Brodie had done the next best thing. He'd vowed to make Willow Creek the most successful ranch in Deaf Smith County. Over the years, no thanks to Rafe and Kenny, Brodie had achieved that goal.

Willow Creek could now boast over three hundred head of cattle and four hundred sheep. His hay crop was phenomenal, his business acumen legendary. Last year, when most farms and ranches struggled to break even, Willow Creek had cleared over one hundred thousand dollars in profit. Brodie Trueblood had indeed done Gil Hollis proud.

Yes, he'd accomplished what he'd first set out to do at the naive age of fourteen. He'd been interested in the operation from the very beginning, spending most of his spare time with the ranch foreman, Cooter Gates. He learned about cattle and hay and what it meant to be a good rancher. By age eighteen, the year his mother died of leukemia, Brodie was running the ranch, while Rafe and Kenny spent their time in honky-tonks and pool halls, living off the sweat of his brow.

The light turned green, and Brodie accelerated. He'd thrown so much of himself into Willow Creek, he'd had no time for a personal life. Now, at twenty-nine, Brodie Trueblood found himself wondering what it would be like to have his own wife and kids. For the first time ever, he was jealous of Kenny. Jealous and angry at the way his older brother mistreated his family blessings.

Would he ever find a good woman to love? A kind, tender woman like his mother. A woman who would cherish Willow Creek as much as he did. A woman who longed for children and a stable home life.

Oddly enough, the image of that redheaded girl back at the bar flitted through his mind.

Don't be ridiculous, Brodie, he chided himself. *She might be good enough for a roll in the hay, but you need to get tangled up with that sort of female the way you need a frontal lobotomy.*

The stack of poker chips in front of Deannie kept growing.

Teasing derision had turned to grudging respect as she won hand after hand. For fifteen years she'd sat in her tiny bedroom way into the wee hours of the night shuffling, dealing, learning the rules. For fifteen years, she'd followed her father from bars to honky-tonks to back alley gambling parlors, and she'd absorbed everything like a sponge, thirsty for the key to her revenge. For fifteen years, she'd thought of only one thing—winning Willow Creek Ranch back from those good-for-nothing Truebloods.

Deannie Hollis had come here with a mission, but suddenly she discovered she was also having fun. It was worth every ounce of effort she'd put into perfecting her skills to watch the look on Kenny's face as he lost again and again. Her only regret—that Rafe Trueblood wasn't the one sitting beside her.

"Where'd you learn to play poker like that, girly?" Lou grumbled, drumming his hammy fingers on the table and frowning at her over his fan of cards.

"My daddy taught me."

"Who's your daddy? Bet we know him."

"Er…" Deannie hesitated, scrambling to invent a fictitious name. "Joe McCellan."

Lou shook his head. "You ever heard of the guy, Kenny?"

"No, but I'm sure Rafe knew him. Where did you say you were from, Deannie?" Kenny angled her a glance. She could feel heat from his gaze as he studied her.

"Amarillo. How many cards do you want?" Deannie asked, grateful for an excuse to change the subject. She was terrified they would catch her in a lie.

"I'm tapped out." One man threw down his cards in disgust.

"Me, too." Another player nodded.

"Too rich for my blood," added a third.

"I'll take four cards," Lou said.

Deannie swung her gaze to Kenny. Her pulse sped up. She hadn't expected to win the ranch back in one game. She knew it would take time and probably a lot more liquor than was currently swirling in Kenny's bloodstream. She'd already taken him for seven hundred dollars. Not a bad start.

"Well, Mr. Trueblood?"

Kenny laid his cards facedown on the table. "Thanks to your phenomenal card-playing abilities, I'm afraid I'm out of money, Miss McCellan."

Her bottom lip twitched. She couldn't let him get away,

not this easily. "You could always put something up for collateral."

"What's my watch worth?" he asked, turning his wrist over. His eyes widened. "Glory, look at the time. I'd better get on to the hospital before Patsy Ann dominoes."

Deannie laid a hand on Kenny's. He looked up. Their eyes met.

"Play one more hand," she urged.

"Why, so you can totally clean me out, watch and all?"

"Oh, right. You're a rich man, Mr. Trueblood. I'd bet what you've lost this evening is mere pocket change."

"Then you'd lose that bet, Miss McCellan." Kenny arched an eyebrow in a sardonic expression.

Deannie threw back her head and laughed. "Please, don't pull my leg, Mr. Trueblood. I've seen your family homestead. I'm sure your father left you sitting pretty."

"So that's your game." Kenny nodded. "I figured you were up to something."

"I don't know what you mean."

"Come on, it's obvious the way you play cards that you've been hustling us."

She fluttered her eyelashes. "A girl has to make a living. So are you in or are you out? I take cars, boats, even ranches."

"I hate to tell you this, darlin', but if you're gold diggin', you're barking up the wrong Trueblood. The old man left the whole kit and caboodle to my little brother, Brodie."

Chapter Two

Brodie Trueblood was a horse of a different color.

Deannie gnawed a thumbnail, chewing off her Cherry Delight fingernail polish. She sat in the parking lot outside the Lonesome Dove, over two thousand dollars in cash resting in her lap, but her victory was hollow. No matter how well she played cards she would never be able to entice Brodie Trueblood into gambling. She'd sensed that about the man from the moment she'd clapped eyes on him.

The sun dipped toward the western horizon. Long shadows slanted across the parking lot. Car doors slammed and cowboys laughed as more people arrived. Deannie could hear the steady throbbing beat from the jukebox as the front door opened again and again.

What now? Where did she go from here? Fifteen years of hard work shot straight down the tubes. A lump of emotion dammed her throat at the thought her plans had been for naught.

"Rafe Trueblood, you son of a gun, why did you have to die before I got here?" Deannie spoke aloud.

There had to be a way to get to Brodie. If not through

gambling, then something else. She would discover his weakness and exploit it, because Deannie would not rest until Willow Creek Ranch once more belonged to a Hollis.

But how?

Deannie caught a glimpse of herself in the rearview mirror. To be social, she'd had a beer while playing cards. The alcohol blushed her cheeks with a faint rosy glow. She had repeatedly raked her hand through her hair, and now her auburn tresses tumbled down her shoulders in hedonistic disarray.

Many men had praised her beauty, telling her she looked exactly like the actress Nicole Kidman, only shorter, but Deannie had never felt comfortable with her appearance or their compliments. In her heart, she was still that gawky freckle faced tomboy in braids. She believed that men, especially Kenny Trueblood types, dished up flattery like candy, hoping to entice gullible females into their beds. Hadn't Daddy constantly warned her to protect her virtue at all costs?

What if she used her looks to attract Brodie Trueblood?

The thought was unexpected but logical. Although Brodie was quite different from his father and brother, he was still a man. A man who could be charmed by the wiles of a woman determined to get what was hers—Willow Creek Ranch.

"Are you seriously thinking about marrying Brodie Trueblood?" Deannie spoke to her image in the mirror. Because nothing short of marrying him would achieve her goal. A strange sensation raced through her at the thought. Married to that potent male?

She could divorce him later, Deannie rationalized. The judge might be inclined to give her the ranch in the divorce settlement when he discovered she was really Deanna Hollis. Her hands trembled. Did she dare do something so bold?

"It's the only answer," she said, excitement building in

her at the prospect. But how did she go about getting Brodie Trueblood to propose marriage?

She needed a plan. For one thing, she had to place herself in his vicinity. Repeatedly. How was she going to accomplish that task?

Starting her ten-year-old Ford sedan, the only possession her father had left her after he'd shot himself six months ago, Deannie pulled out of the parking lot, her mind racing.

Brodie had probably gone to the hospital to be with his sister-in-law, she surmised. Or else he'd returned home to Willow Creek. Either way, she couldn't go wrong heading toward the ranch.

On her way out of town, Deannie drove through a poverty-stricken neighborhood. Threading her way through crooked back streets, she finally found what she was looking for.

A homeless shelter. Still there after fifteen years. The place where she and Daddy had taken refuge the first night Rafe Trueblood had thrown them from their home.

Vividly she remembered the horror of that night, clutching Daddy's hand as he led her here to this dark, scary place that smelled of boiled cabbage and old sweat socks. They'd been served overcooked stew and stale corn bread. She and Daddy had slept together on a mattress on the cement floor. Deannie had sucked her thumb and cried for her ruffled, pink canopy bed and her Shetland pony, Hero.

Rafe Trueblood had been responsible. It was all his fault they were on the streets, and life had never been the same again. That's when her burning hatred had begun.

Fighting back tears, Deannie got out of the car, dashed up the uneven steps in the gathering darkness and banged on the door. Paint, once white, now a dingy gray, peeled off the side of the building in long strips.

"Yes?" said the elderly woman with a beatific smile who answered her knock. "May I help you?"

"Do you work here?" Deannie asked.

"I'm Ester Sweeny, the director. Are you in need, child?"

"No. I want to help." Taking a deep breath, Deannie shoved the money she'd taken from the men at the poker game into the woman's startled hands.

"My goodness, dear, are you sure? This is a lot of money."

But Deannie was already flying down the steps, her breath coming in spurts. She drove away without looking back.

It was near midnight by the time Brodie Trueblood turned off the highway and onto the graveled road leading home. A satisfied smile rested on his lips. Patsy Ann had done well, bringing another Trueblood into the world. Phillip Brodie. Seven pounds, eight ounces, and in full possession of a great pair of lungs.

And even Kenny had finally shown up, just in time to take Brodie's place in the delivery room. Grudgingly, Brodie gave his older brother credit for that at least.

Yawning, Brodie turned the corner. His headlights reflected off a car parked on the shoulder of the road. The hood was raised. Brodie slowed, squinting into the darkness. He didn't recognize the car as belonging to a neighbor.

Someone stepped from the shadows. A woman. She raised her arms, shielding her eyes against his high-beam lights.

Brodie braked and veered off the road. Leaving his engine idling, he got out.

"You all right, ma'am?" he asked as he walked back to her stalled vehicle.

"Thank heavens you stopped," she said, her voice reedy in the cool evening air. She moved toward him. "I thought I'd be stranded here all night."

"Not too many people live on this road," he acknowledged. "You visiting someone?" The clouds rolled away from the moon, bathing the road in a silvery shimmer.

The woman shook her head, her hair tumbling sexily about her shoulders. Her skin glowed ethereally in the gossamer moonlight. She looked like a fairy sprite.

"No." She shook her head and her curls danced bewitchingly. "I'm afraid I took a wrong turn and then my car conked out."

Something about her was familiar. Frowning, Brodie tilted his head. She stood a few feet from him, shivering slightly, her arms crossed over her chest.

"Are you cold?" he asked.

"A little."

Brodie unbuttoned his flannel shirt.

"Oh, please, you don't have to give me your shirt."

"No trouble. I've got a T-shirt on underneath," he said, stripping the garment off and handing it to her. Tentatively she took his shirt and shrugged into it.

"Thank you." The sleeves dangled way past her hands, giving her a lost-little-girl appearance.

"Do I know you?" He studied her face in the moonlight. They were so close he could smell her scent, sweet as magnolias and twice as nice.

"I'm Deannie McCellan," she said, extending her hand.

Her palm felt so soft in his own. Soft and warm and pleasant. "Nice to meet you, Ms. McCellan. I'm Brodie Trueblood," he said, surprised to find that his words hung in his throat.

"Brodie Trueblood, hmm, I think we have met, but we weren't formally introduced."

He stared into her eyes, mesmerized. "At the Lonesome Dove."

"That's right." She smiled.

Unnerved, Brodie realized he was still holding on to her hand. Embarrassed, he let go and took a step back. "You were with my brother, Kenny."

"I was merely playing cards with him and his friends," she corrected. "I think you got the wrong impression."

"Oh, no...I mean...I didn't think...oh, hell." Brodie swept his cowboy hat off his head. "I didn't mean to imply any relationship between you and Kenny. I was just mad at him."

"No need to apologize." She smiled so brightly Brodie feared he might melt under the intensity.

"Not meaning to be rude, but what's a lady like you hanging out with guys like my brother and his friends?"

"Everybody has to let off some steam now and then. The fellas invited me to play cards with them and I thought, What the heck?"

"I see." Except he didn't see at all. As far as Brodie was concerned, ladies had no place in establishments like the Lonesome Dove, but he was too polite to say so.

He shifted his weight, settled his hat back on his head. "What seems to be wrong with your car, ma'am?"

"Please," she whispered, "call me Deannie."

"Okay. Deannie."

She shook her head. "I don't know. I'm completely hopeless when it comes to anything mechanical. One minute I was driving along, the next thing I knew the car started to clatter and shake and simply stopped."

"Were you able to steer it?"

"No. That's why I'm parked in such a haphazard manner." She indicated the car with a wave.

"Could be the drive shaft," Brodie mused, stroking his jaw with a thumb and forefinger.

"Is that bad?"

"It's not good."

Deannie sighed. "Oh, my, I hope it doesn't cost a lot. I don't have much money."

"The fellas at the bar clean you out?"

"I'm afraid so."

"Don't mean to tell you how to run your business, but believe me, gambling is a habit that only leads to trouble."

"Oh, I don't indulge often." She batted her eyelashes at him, and Brodie had the strangest feeling that Deannie McCellan was gambling right at that very moment.

"Guess that remark was outta line, but my daddy was a professional gambler, and my brother seems to be following in his footsteps. I know first-hand how ruinous it can be."

"Well, Mr. Trueblood, I appreciate your concern."

Was she making fun of him? It was hard to read her expression in the dim moonlight.

"I could take a look at your car tonight, but truthfully, it would be better to wait until morning. One of my ranch hands is also a mechanic. He could probably fix it for the cost of parts."

"Do you really think so? That would be great."

"Is there someone I can call for you?" Brodie asked, disturbed by the feelings this woman stirred in him.

"I don't know anyone in this part of the country. I was on my way to a job interview in Santa Fe."

"Oh." So she was unemployed.

Watch out, Brodie, the voice in the back of his head warned. *There's something not quite right about this gorgeous filly. She's not at all what she seems.*

"Yeah, I sound like a great security risk. No job, no money, a broken-down car." Deannie laughed.

The rich, throaty sound affected Brodie viscerally. Before he knew what he was doing, he found himself offering to take her home. "You can come to my ranch with me. I've got several empty guests rooms, and you're more than welcome. We'll worry about the car first thing tomorrow morning."

"That's so generous of you to offer, but I can't possibly put you out like that." She pursed her full lips, and it bothered Brodie that he couldn't take his eyes off her mouth.

"What would your wife say about you bringing home a stranger?"

"I'm not married."

"Oh. I suppose that's even a stronger reason for me to decline your kind invitation. We wouldn't want to set local tongues waggin'. After all, you've got to live here."

"Don't worry about that. The Truebloods keep the Deaf Smith County gossips in business. We're more reliable than the newsstand tabloids."

Deannie smiled. "Well, if you're sure."

"I swear it's no problem."

"Then I accept."

Her acceptance felt like a gift, and it shouldn't have. Why had he asked her to stay? Was he insane, tempting fate like this? She'd been hanging out in a bar with Kenny for heaven's sake. Brodie couldn't deny his attraction to her, but common sense cautioned him not to get tangled up with this woman. But what else could he do? He wasn't about to leave her here all night. It was twenty miles back to Yarborough, and he had to be up at five-thirty. She would stay one night. No big deal. Rory would fix her car tomorrow, and she would be on her way. End of story. He need never explore this unexpected fascination with Deannie McCellan.

"Let me get my stuff from the car."

Brodie waited while she opened the trunk and retrieved a duffel bag and her purse.

"All set?"

She grinned, reappearing at his elbow, her intoxicating magnolia aroma filling his nose and making him think of white lace wedding gowns and diamond engagement rings. Swallowing hard, Brodie escorted her to the passenger side of his pickup truck, pondering the sudden acceleration of his pulse.

Sliding under the wheel, he put the truck in gear and headed for home. Silence reverberated in the small cab.

Brodie cleared his throat, racking his brain for something to say.

"So," Deannie said, "did Kenny's wife have her baby?"

"Yeah." Brodie smiled in spite of himself. "Another boy. Phillip Brodie."

"She named him after you?"

"It was nice of her."

"I'm sure you deserve the honor."

Her comment embarrassed him. "I don't know about that."

"I am. Any man gallant enough to rescue a bar dolly with a broken-down car in the middle of the night is a true gentleman."

"I'm sorry about that 'bar dolly' crack." Grateful for the cover of darkness, Brodie felt his face flame red.

"I've been called much worse," Deannie assured him.

"Not within my hearing." The idea of someone verbally abusing her sent anger coursing through his whole system. Why did he feel so protective of her?

"See. You are a true gentleman."

Brodie squirmed in the seat. "Guess I am sort of old-fashioned."

"I find it refreshing."

Up ahead Brodie spotted the security lights of Willow Creek. He'd never been so glad to see the place in his entire life. "Here we are," he said, turning into the long drive-way.

Was it his imagination or did Deannie catch her breath as she peered out the window at the grounds?

"All this is yours?" she asked.

"Yep. My daddy died two weeks ago and left the ranch to me. But I've been running it for years. If it hadn't been for me, my old man would have gambled the place away years ago."

"You're very lucky."

There was no denying the sarcasm in her voice. Was she jealous? She had no right to be. He'd earned everything he'd achieved through hard, honest work, and he didn't appreciate what her sarcasm implied.

"Willow Creek is my life." He spoke more sharply than he'd intended. Deannie's face was turned away from him, but he noticed she held her shoulders stiff, unbending. "I've never loved anything the way I love this land."

"I can understand that feeling," she said, her words muffled.

"Can you?" Brodie pulled up in front of the house and killed the engine. He looked over at Deannie but she didn't answer him. "Come on," he said, "I'll show you to your room."

Curiously, Deannie's heart slowed until she feared it might stop beating altogether. After fifteen years, she'd finally come home.

Following Brodie through the back door and into the kitchen, she fought the assault of memories tumbling through her mind.

Her vision narrowed, and the past rushed at her. She remembered running in and out of that same door until her mama, pressing Daddy's shirts at the ironing board, had hollered at her to come inside or stay outside. And the kitchen! When Brodie flicked on the overhead light, Deannie sucked in her breath at the shock of seeing it again. The color of the walls was different and so were the furnishings, but it was the kitchen she'd known. She had sat in that spot by the bay window and eaten her breakfast, watching birds at the feeder in the mesquite trees. Her mother had washed Deannie's hair in that sink, had baked cookies in that oven, had stocked canned goods in that pantry. Deannie even fancied she could smell Mama's clean, wholesome scent, a combination of soap, peaches and homemade bread.

Blood drained from her face, and she suddenly felt very cold. She hugged herself. Perspiration dampened her forehead, and she feared she might faint.

"Deannie?"

Brodie's voice came to her from a fog. She shook her head.

His arm went around her waist, strong but gentle. "Are you all right?" His mouth was so close to her ear. "Here, sit down."

Obediently she sank into the chair he pulled out for her.

"Have you eaten today?" he demanded.

"Peanuts. At the bar," she murmured, surprised at how weak her limbs felt.

Brodie snorted. "And I suppose you were drinking, too."

"Just one beer."

"On an empty stomach." He clicked his tongue and turned his back on her to rummage through the refrigerator. "Actually, I got so wrapped up in coaching Patsy Ann, I didn't eat any supper, either. Matilda will probably hit the roof, but we're raiding the fridge."

"Matilda?" Brodie had said he wasn't married, but what if he had a live-in girlfriend? An emotion, curiously like jealousy stabbed through her. Surely she wasn't jealous. No, she was just worried about competition for his affections. Getting rid of a girlfriend would add to the complexity of her marriage scheme.

"Matilda Jennings is my current housekeeper."

"She gets mad when you raid your own refrigerator?"

"Matilda's not one for cleaning up messes."

"So why do you keep her on as housekeeper?"

"Out here in the sticks, housekeepers aren't so easy to come by. And ever since Patsy Ann and the kids moved in, Matilda's been particularly testy." He chuckled.

"At least you have a sense of humor about it."

Brodie shrugged. "'Fraid I can't see any other way to approach the situation."

He hauled out a platter of roast beef, sliced purple onions, a jar of mayonnaise, lettuce, tomatoes, pickles and olives. Retrieving a loaf of whole wheat from the bread basket on the counter, he then sat the food on the table. Stomach growling, Deannie watched as he made sandwiches and poured two glasses of milk.

"Try that," he said, sliding a glass plate in front of her.

"Oh, my," Deannie said, sinking her teeth into the sandwich. It tasted like heaven. Just the kind of hearty sandwich her mother used to create.

Brodie winked. "Unless I miss my guess, I think we have chocolate chip cookies for dessert."

Deannie met his gaze and stopped chewing. She was wearing his shirt and it smelled of him, the soft material rubbing against her skin. It was as if he had enveloped her in a massive bear hug.

Under the scrutiny of bright lights, the man was even more handsome than she'd imagined. He possessed a long, firm jawline and a straight nose. He doffed his cowboy hat and settled it into the chair beside him. A ridge ringed his dark hair where the hat left its imprint. He smiled at her and his light brown eyes crinkled at the corners. Something tugged deep within her, something dangerous and exciting.

They both dropped their gazes at the same time.

Get a grip on your emotions, Deannie, she cautioned herself. His handsomeness would make the chore of winning his affections less odious, but she must never forget he was a Trueblood. She'd come to Willow Creek with an express mission in mind—to win back her home, one way or the other. If she couldn't gamble the place out from under Kenny Trueblood, then she would seduce it out of Brodie. But she would have to be darned careful not to lose her heart in the bargain.

"That was delicious," she said, wiping her hands on a paper napkin. "Thank you."

"You're welcome." He ducked his head, looking all the world like a shy little boy, and Deannie had to suppress an overwhelming urge to muss his hair.

"Let me help you with that." Scraping back her chair, she started collecting leftovers.

"Just dump the dirty dishes in the sink."

"And risk making Matilda mad?"

"It's too late to be worrying about washing dishes," Brodie said firmly. He took the plates from her hands. Their fingers brushed lightly. Brodie jumped back as if scalded, dropping a plate to the floor. It shattered, sending splinters flying across the hardwood floor.

"Damn," he swore.

"I'll get the broom," Deannie said, and without thinking, stepped into the anteroom and opened the broom closet. She turned around to find Brodie standing behind her.

"How did you know where the broom closet was?" he asked.

"Lucky guess," Deannie said nervously. Whew, boy, she would have to watch herself. She hadn't thought twice about her actions, heading instinctively for the broom closet. Another stupid mistake like that one and she would tip her hand for sure. "A lot of these old farmhouses have similar floor plans."

Brodie said nothing, but a suspicious gleam lit his eyes, and he pressed his lips firmly together. Taking the broom and dustpan from her, he silently swept up the glass.

"I'll show you to your room," he said, dumping the glass in the trash can and returning the utensils to the broom closet.

Deannie gathered up her duffel bag and purse and followed Brodie upstairs. The hallway was lit by a series of night-lights. The old floorboards creaked under their

weight. It looked like home and yet it was not. The Truebloods had carved their mark in her family homestead. The
wallpaper was different, as was the carpet. And the house
smelled of Brodie—masculine, outdoorsy—leather and hay
and sunshine.

What was he thinking? Deannie fretted, watching his
shoulders sway. His mood had changed in the kitchen.
Could he possibly have guessed her true identity? If so,
why didn't he confront her?

He led her past the master bedroom where her parents
used to sleep. Her old room was next door. But Brodie
didn't stop there. He took her down the hall to the last
bedroom on the right.

"I'm sure you'll be comfortable here," he said rather
stiffly. "Now, if you'll excuse me, I'm going to bed. I've
got to be up in four hours."

"Yes. Thanks."

Turning, he sauntered back toward the master bedroom.
Deannie opened the door and switched on the light. This
had once been her mother's sewing room. The old sewing
machine had stood near the window where a full-size oak
bedroom suite now sat. Her mother had spent many hours
here making Deannie's dresses. Stacks of material, boxes
of thread, yards of lace had decorated the shelf that currently held books and various knickknacks.

A fierce nostalgia swept through her. A vivid longing for
what used to be. She owed it to herself, to her parents, to
reclaim what was rightfully hers. Her memories were here,
her history, her past. Her future.

Changing from Brodie's work shirt and her silky dress
into a blue cotton nightgown, Deannie padded across the
hall to the bathroom where she brushed her teeth and
washed the makeup from her face. Once finished, she returned to her bedroom, shut the door and slipped between
the cool sheets.

Her body was tired, but her mind raced, fully alert. Disabling her car on the roadside had been a stroke of genius. Thank heavens no one else had driven by before Brodie.

The plot had worked wonderfully. The stalled vehicle had gotten her in the door, now it was up to her to turn up the heat under the sizzle that Lady Luck had created between the two of them. For there was no denying the natural attraction that snapped from her to Brodie and back again. The broken plate testified to that.

Coming home to Willow Creek, seeing the ranch again after fifteen years, served to solidify her resolve. She had to get it back. And if that meant she would have to marry Brodie Trueblood to accomplish her goals, then that's what she would do. Deannie Hollis could think of far worse fates.

Had Deannie lied about her association with Kenny? Brodie wondered. He rolled over in bed, cupped the back of his head in his palms and stared at the ceiling. How had she known about the broom closet? Had she and Kenny been using the farmhouse as their trysting place whenever he was away?

Cringing at the thought of his brother and Deannie having an illicit affair in one of these bedrooms, Brodie bit down on his bottom lip to stifle a groan. He hated to believe it, but the truth was he'd found her in a bar playing poker with Kenny. That didn't speak well of her character.

Judge not, least ye be judged.

His mother's favorite biblical quote floated through his head. How many times had she recited that phrase when he'd railed against his father's reprehensible behavior? Even on her deathbed the woman had never uttered one condemning word. Brodie was not so forgiving. From his viewpoint, Rafe Trueblood was a good-for-nothing scoundrel.

But what about Deannie McCellan? Was it pure coincidence that she'd made a wrong turn and her car had stalled on the road to Willow Creek? Or had she been hoping to rendezvous with Kenny? Had his brother kissed those full sweet lips right here in this house? Had his hands caressed Deannie's skin, kneaded her breasts. Oh, God! Why did the thought cause his gut to burn, his chest to tighten?

Because he didn't want to see Kenny treating Patsy Ann the way his father had treated his mother, Brodie told himself. That was why. He felt no jealousy. None at all. How could he be jealous when he didn't even know the woman?

Yet there was something about Deannie McCellan. The calm serenity in those pale blue eyes, the sheen of her auburn hair, the regal way she carried herself, captured his imagination the way no female had in a very long time. When they had been in the kitchen together, eating sandwiches, he'd had the most overpowering urge to lean over and kiss her. Merely brushing her fingertips had caused him to bust that plate.

Could it be he was just anxious to get involved in a relationship, and Deannie McCellan happened to be in the right place at the right time? Sighing, Brodie flopped over onto his side. No. It was more than that. He felt an odd emotion he couldn't explain. Something he'd never really experienced before. Something that told him she might be the one he'd been waiting for these past few years.

Proceed with caution, Trueblood. No point jumping the gun. Especially when your heart's on the line. The last thing you need is to get mixed up with a female version of Rafe!

Chapter Three

The aroma of strong coffee tugged open Deannie's eyelids at 6:00 a.m. Habit urged her to roll over and go back to sleep, but one name popped into her mind, settling the issue.

Brodie Trueblood.

Flinging the covers aside, Deannie sat up. She had to make the most of the morning. As soon as Brodie's ranch hand inspected her car and discovered nothing wrong with it, she would have no excuse for lingering at Willow Creek. Time was of the essence. She must secure Brodie's interest in her today.

Never an early riser, she yawned, stretched and rubbed her eyes. "Come on, Deannie, get it in gear," she mumbled. Changing into jeans and a red cotton blouse, she took a deep breath to fortify herself before putting on sneakers and heading downstairs.

Childish voices drifted from the kitchen.

"When's Mama comin' home, Unc' Brodie?"

"Maybe this afternoon."

"Thank heavens," a woman muttered.

"With our new baby brother?" the child chirped.

"Uh-huh."

Oddly enough, Brodie's voice sent shivers skipping down Deannie's spine. She peeked around the corner into the kitchen and surveyed the scene before her.

A tall, middle-aged woman stood at the sink scrubbing dishes, her steel gray curls shaking with movement, her mouth pressed into a hard, uncompromising line.

Brodie sat at the table, two children in his lap. A blond girl of about three was tucked into the crook of his left arm. The boy, slightly older and the spitting image of Kenny Trueblood, was nestled on his right.

"Who's her?" The little boy pointed a finger at Deannie.

"Probably the one who messed up my kitchen last night," the woman at the sink said, turning to glare at Deannie. No doubt this was the infamous Matilda.

"Good morning," Brodie greeted her, a smile on his face. "Come have breakfast with us."

Deannie returned his smile and wriggled her fingers.

"Yeah, come on in." Matilda heaved a sigh. "Doesn't matter that I just got through feeding the ranch hands."

"Matilda, Miss McCellan is our guest. I trust you'll remember that," Brodie said curtly to the surly housekeeper.

"Don't go to any trouble. Cereal is fine with me," Deannie said politely. What she really wanted to do was tell the old witch to stuff her rotten attitude.

"Good," Matilda huffed. "Corn flakes are in the pantry."

Feeling like a pariah, Deannie inched past Matilda, took corn flakes from the pantry, a bowl from the cupboard and milk from the refrigerator, then settled in across the table from Brodie and the kids.

"You pretty," the girl announced. "Whatcha name?"

"I'm Deannie and you're very pretty, too."

The little girl beamed. "I knowed."

"This is Angel," Brodie said, tweaking the child's hair. "And this one here is Richard, but we all call him Buster."

"Hi," Deannie said, unnerved by the kids. She hadn't been around children much, wasn't sure how to deal with them, but she had a feeling if she could charm the little tykes she might be able to melt Uncle Brodie's heart. And melting Brodie Trueblood's heart was number one on her agenda of things to do today.

"Sleep well?" Brodie asked, feeding Angel a toast diamond.

"Not long enough." Deannie gave him a wry smile. "I'm afraid I'm not much of an early bird."

"You gotta stop hanging out in bars."

Was he teasing or warning her? Deannie studied his face, unsure of his meaning.

"You're right, a girl can pick up some very bad habits in those places."

"At the very least."

Their gazes welded. Brodie didn't blink. Deannie gulped.

"This job you're applying for in New Mexico, it's in a bar, isn't it?" he asked.

Deannie had almost forgotten about the white lie she'd told him the night before. "Guilty."

Brodie nodded grimly, and Deannie had a feeling she'd just made a grave tactical error. "I'll tow your car into the yard. Whenever Rory can spare a few minutes from his regular chores this morning, I'll have him take a look at it."

"Thank you."

"I know you'd like to be on your way as soon as possible."

Was that a hint? Did he want her gone? Well, too bad, she wasn't surrendering that easily.

"No hurry. I wouldn't want to cause an inconvenience."

"Hop up, kids, I've got work to do." Brodie eased Angel and Buster from his lap. Getting to his feet, he took his straw cowboy hat from a peg on the wall and settled it onto his head.

He cut a dashing figure. The epitome of a West Texas cowboy, in his faded jeans and well-worn work boots. He looked like he belonged riding the range at Willow Creek.

That idea startled Deannie. Truthfully, she'd never thought beyond getting even with Rafe Trueblood, but she had to consider the fact that Brodie might actually love this ranch as much as she did.

Unbidden, her eyes took in his firmly muscled forearms peeking from beneath rolled-up shirtsleeves. His top two shirt buttons were undone, and she could see tufts of curly black hair just begging to be caressed. Clenching her jaw, Deannie quickly looked away before Brodie spotted raw desire in her eyes.

He'd started out the door when the phone rang. Matilda answered, then called to him. "It's for you," she said, dangling the receiver from one work-roughened finger.

Treading back across the room, he favored Deannie with another whiff of his special scent. This morning he smelled of soap and bacon, toothpaste and coffee. Deannie took a bite of corn flakes and tried not to notice. She realized both kids were staring at her with unabashed interest.

"Hello?" he spoke into the phone.

She didn't mean to eavesdrop, but she was sitting right at Brodie's elbow. Short of clamping her hands over her ears, she was forced to listen to the conversation.

"Patsy Ann. How's my favorite sister-in-law this morning?"

"It's Mama!" Buster exclaimed, jumping up and down. "I wanna talk to her."

"Me too, me too," Angel squealed.

"Honey, why are you crying?" A concerned expression folded Brodie's mouth into a straight line. "Calm down now, I can't understand you."

"Mama," Buster whined, reaching for the phone.

Brodie waved a hand for silence.

Deannie placed an index finger to her lip. "Shhh," she whispered to Buster. "Let Uncle Brodie talk to your mama."

Buster stared at her. "No!" he announced, wrapping his arms around his uncle's leg and burying his face against his hip.

"Nice try," Brodie mouthed to Deannie. She had a sudden urge to slink off into the corner.

"What's that? An infection?" Brodie returned his attention to Patsy Ann. "I'm sorry to hear that. The doctor says you've got to stay at the hospital for a few more days?"

"She's my mama, too," Angel wailed.

"Oh, no," Matilda erupted, throwing her hands into the air. "I'm not taking care of these brats any longer. It's not my job."

Glaring at Matilda, Brodie bent down and scooped a sobbing Buster into his arms. "Is the baby okay? Good. Don't worry about Buster and Angel. I'll hold down the fort."

Matilda clanged a pan against the sink for emphasis. Tears drizzled down Angel's cheeks.

"Is Kenny there?" Brodie spoke into the receiver.

Apparently Patsy Ann answered in the negative, because Brodie turned his head and swore softly under his breath.

Poor Brodie. He had an irresponsible brother on the loose, a hysterical sister-in-law on the phone, two crying kids clinging to him and a witchy housekeeper dishing out grief. For the first time in her life Deannie actually felt sorry for a Trueblood.

"Here, Buster, talk to your mama."

Face flushed with fury, Brodie handed the phone to his nephew and set him on the bar. Whirling on his heels, he stalked across the kitchen to confront Matilda.

"You're fired," he said. "Now."

Matilda crossed her arms over her chest. "Fine with me.

You've been impossible to please ever since your sister-in-law and those kids moved in here.''

"Out!" he thundered, pointing a finger at the door. "You've got four hours to collect your things and be gone.''

With a toss of her head, Matilda haughtily sailed out of the room.

Slumping down in the chair beside Deannie, Brodie lowered his head and plowed fingers through his hair. "What am I going to do now?" he muttered. "I've got a ranch to run. I don't have time to watch two preschoolers.''

Fate had dropped a plum into her lap. Last night's emergency plan with the stalled car had only been a temporary solution. This current situation, however, offered her prime opportunity to be close to Brodie for several days. Long enough to fuel his interest in her.

Deannie cleared her throat.

Brodie raised his eyes.

"We could strike a bargain," she said. "You scratch my back, I'll scratch yours.''

One eyebrow lifted on his forehead.

Steepling her fingers, Deannie took a deep breath. Would he take the bait? "Fix my car, Brodie Trueblood, and I'll watch the kids and keep house for you until Patsy Ann is out of the hospital.''

No. Definitely not. Bad idea. A disaster waiting to happen. Brodie knew he could not stay under the same roof with this bewitching woman for the next two or three days completely unchaperoned except for children. He knew absolutely nothing about Deannie McCellan save for the fact she roused him to distracting heights, and for all he knew, she was very possibly his brother's mistress.

He stared at Deannie. Was that why she wanted the job? To get closer to Kenny? Did she think by playing nurse-maid to his kids, she would worm her way into his brother's heart and he would divorce his wife? If that was her plan, she was way off beam. Kenny rarely put in an appearance at Willow Creek. In fact, he hadn't been around since Rafe's funeral, when Patsy Ann and the kids had moved in.

Deannie's eyes, the pale blue of his stock pond in a winter freeze, widened.

"I...er...well," Brodie stammered, unsure of how to refuse her offer.

"I want down," Buster hollered. "Mama hung up."

Brodie got to his feet, grateful for the distraction, and retrieved Buster from the counter. Settling the telephone receiver back in its cradle, he glanced over and saw Angel standing in a chair, her fingers in the margarine tub.

"Oh, no," he groaned as she stuck a handful into her mouth. "Angel, stop that."

"I wike butter." His niece gave him a greasy yellow smile.

Brodie swung his gaze to Deannie. She sat with her hands folded demurely in her lap, a serene expression on her face. Ha! These two hellions would erase that smug smile from her lips in nothing flat.

"You're hired," Brodie said, sitting Buster on the floor and reaching for Angel. "Could you get me a wet rag, please?"

Okay, so she wasn't domestic. That didn't mean she was completely helpless. Did it?

Deannie glanced at the two round-faced children staring at her. What now? No wonder Brodie had looked extremely relieved when he'd headed out the back door. Oh well, nothing to do but roll up her sleeves and plunge right in. If she wanted to convince Brodie Trueblood she was the marrying kind, she would have to prove she could manage a house and kids.

"What do you guys usually do after breakfast?" she asked.

"Watch TV!" Buster giggled.

"Play in mud!" Angel squealed.

Three and five years old and already con artists. No denying these two were Truebloods.

A thought occurred to Deannie. Something that would keep the kids occupied and allow her to explore the house that had once been her home at the same time.

"You kids ever play hide-and-seek?"

"Yeah," Buster said, wriggling his little hips with excitement.

"No." Angel shook her head.

"Yes you have, 'member?" Buster scoffed.

"Nuh-uh."

He shoved his sister. Angel slugged him with a tiny fist.

"Stop it! Right now," Deannie commanded. "If you don't straighten up, it's naptime for both of you."

"You can't make us." Buster defiantly folded his chubby arms across his chest, raised his chin and glared at her.

"Yeah. You not our mama." Angel backed her brother.

"Your Uncle Brodie left me in charge. So let's get something straight. Whatever I say goes." Deannie shook an index finger for emphasis. "If you're nice to me, I'll be nice to you. If not..."

"What?" Buster challenged.

Yeah, Deannie, what? Casting in her mind, Deannie tried to remember her own childhood punishments. "You'll have to stand in the corner for five minutes."

"Let's play hide-and-seek," Angel wheedled, pushing blond curls from her face. "'Kay, Buster?"

Buster relaxed his stance, dropped his arms. "Okay."

"Let's go upstairs to play," Deannie urged. She was dying to get a peek in Brodie's room. The very bedroom that had once belonged to Gil and Francie Hollis.

"All right," Deannie said, after they trooped upstairs. "This chair in the hall is base. I'll sit here, close my eyes and count to one hundred while you guys go hide. You've got to stay hidden until I come looking for you. Then you try to get back to base before I tag you. Understand?"

Angel nodded.

"Yeah, I know how to play." Buster looked bored.

"All set?" Deannie eased herself down in the chair, put her hands over her eyes. "One, two, three, four…"

Giggles and the sound of running feet erupted.

The minute they dispersed, Deannie got to her feet and headed for Brodie's bedroom. "Ten, eleven, hide real good…" she sang out, her heart suddenly racing as her hand closed over the doorknob.

"Twelve, thirteen…" She pushed into the room.

Brodie kept the place exceptionally tidy. No clothes on the floor, no overflowing wastebaskets, no dirty dishes. A bookcase housed a variety of fiction and nonfiction titles. Cowboy paintings decorated the wall. A small writing desk sat in one corner with a state-of-the-art computer system perched on top.

She hadn't really expected to see anything remaining that had once belonged to her parents, but the sight of the huge, four-poster oak bed served to be Deannie's undoing.

Her breath caught in her lungs. A flash of memory shot through her mind. Suddenly she was Buster's age, padding into the room in her pajamas. Mama and Daddy were snuggling together beneath the down quilt. They spotted her and threw back the covers, inviting her to join them. Joy had surged through her as she leaped into the family bed and felt her parents' love surround her.

Deannie gulped. Her face flushed alternately hot, then cold. Tears stung her eyelids. Oh, the sorrow for what she had lost! Her mother. Her father. Her home.

And it was Rafe Trueblood's fault. If he had been there

at that very moment, Deannie would have launched herself at him, attacking him with her bare fists.

"Deannie?" She heard Buster's voice calling to her through the fog enveloping her mind. "You didn't come look for us."

"That's cause she's too busy snooping around in your uncle's bedroom," Matilda said from the doorway, two suitcases clutched in her hands.

Deannie blinked, stared at the angry woman. "The children and I were playing hide-and-seek."

"Don't think I can't see what you're up to," Matilda challenged. "Brodie Trueblood might be a fool, but I ain't."

Without thinking twice, Deannie jumped to Brodie's defense. "Don't you ever call him such a thing."

"You're trying to get your hands on Willow Creek Ranch. I can see it plain as day."

"Don't be ridiculous. I'm just passing through town."

"Are you? You look familiar to me."

"I've never been in Yarborough before in my life."

"So you say."

"My car broke down."

"That's not hard to fake." Matilda snorted.

"Brodie fired you. I offered to watch the kids in exchange for having my car repaired. That's all," Deannie replied coldly, but deep inside her heart Matilda's words struck terror. Had the housekeeper guessed at her true identity? Would she tell Brodie her suspicions in a desperate bid to get her job back?

Matilda's eyes narrowed. "I know your type. Always scheming. You got ways. And don't think I'm not going to be keeping an eye on you, because I am."

"I believe you were headed out the front door."

"Aren't we gonna play anymore?" Buster demanded.

"Yes, honey, we are." Deannie turned her back on the

woman, tried her best to ignore the frantic tripping of her pulse. She took Buster's hand. "Let's go find your sister."

"What's wrong with the car?" Brodie asked Rory Travis, reining in his horse, Ranger, and sliding off the roan's broad back. Tilting his cowboy hat back on his head, he mopped his brow with a bandana, then tied Ranger to the corral gate.

Rory shook his head. "It's the darnedest thing, boss. Can't find a thing amiss."

"Nothing?"

"Starts fine. I took it up and down the road a few times, not a bit of problem."

Brodie angled a look up at the ranch house perched on the hill and pursed his lips. He hated to jump to conclusions, but something about Deannie McCellan didn't ring true. The fact that Rory could find nothing wrong with her car only served to deepen Brodie's conviction that the woman had finagled an overnight invitation to Willow Creek and had ensconced herself in the house until Patsy Ann's return.

Was he attributing her with motives she didn't possess? The part of him that was attracted to Deannie wanted so badly to trust her, yet he knew first-hand how such women operated. How many times had his father been bilked out of money by a pretty face and a shapely figure? No. He could not afford to make such a mistake.

It was time he had a heart-to-heart with his brother and find out just what was going on between him and this woman.

"I'm going into town," Brodie told Rory.

"Okay."

"Keep checking out her car. I'd hate to have the thing die on Deannie halfway between here and Santa Fe."

"Will do." Rory nodded and wiped his grease-stained hands on a red rag pulled from his back pocket.

* * *

Brodie found Kenny at the Lonesome Dove pitching darts.

"Do you ever go home?" he asked his older brother.

"Now and then, when I need a fresh change of clothes," Kenny replied, landing a bull's-eye.

"Did you hear about Patsy Ann's complications?"

"Yeah. I dropped by the hospital about an hour ago."

"Well, bully for you. Have you given any thought to coming to see your kids?"

Kenny looked chagrined. "I guess I need to do that."

"Damned straight you do."

"Okay, I'll come by and pick them up this evening."

"Is that the only reason you'd be coming to Willow Creek?" Brodie glanced sideways at his brother and realized he was hoping against hope Kenny would deny any involvement with Deannie McCellan. Would he believe him if he did?

"What are you talking about?" Kenny threw another dart.

"Your mistress." Brodie pressed his lips tightly together, tried his best to ignore the knot growing in his gut.

"My what?"

"Don't try to deny it."

"Little brother, I don't have a clue what you're talking about."

"Deannie McCellan."

"Who?"

"The woman you played cards with last night."

"Oh, the redhead."

"Yes. Her. You're going to tell me you and she don't have a thing going on?"

"Come on, little brother, I have my faults but I've never cheated on Patsy Ann."

"You think I'm going to buy that? You live just like Rafe. Gambling, drinking, hanging out with losers. You expect me to believe you didn't inherit his womanizing genes, too.''

"I don't have to listen to your crap. You come struttin' in here all high-and-mighty, and expect me to explain myself to you. Just because you like taking the moral high ground doesn't mean you're always right. There's nothing wrong with having a good time.''

Brodie clenched his fists and willed himself not to raise their age-old philosophic differences. "Kenny, tell me the truth. Are you or aren't you having an affair? Is that the real reason Patsy Ann left?''

"I ain't denying I've made a lot of mistakes in my marriage, but I love my wife.''

"You sure have a funny way of showing it.''

"Well dammit, Brodie, you see how she nags. Always trying to change me.''

"With good reason.''

Kenny shrugged. "Believe what you want, but I'm telling you I've never cheated on Patsy Ann.''

"Then what's Deannie McCellan doing at Willow Creek?''

"Maybe she decided you were the better catch.''

"What's that supposed to mean? Do you think she's after me?''

"How would I know?'' Kenny glared. "You're the one who popped up accusing me of things I've never done and with a woman I only met once. Why don't you ask her what she's doing at Willow Creek?''

Stunned, Brodie stared at his brother. Maybe Deannie's story was true. Maybe her car really had broken down. Maybe she *had* been on her way to New Mexico for a job interview. Suddenly he felt guilty for doubting her, and curiously, his heart lightened.

All the way back to the ranch, Brodie pondered his blossoming feelings for Deannie McCellan. She created a burning excitement in him without even trying. From the moment he'd seen her in the bar, something inside him had clicked. And this morning, fresh from her bed, sheet wrinkles still creased into her otherwise flawless skin, she'd caused a distinct stirring below his belt.

Everything about her drove him crazy—her rich, sweet, intoxicating scent, that long red mane flowing about her slender shoulders, those pale blue eyes that seemed to stare straight into his soul. That tight little tush, her soft round breasts, those heavenly legs. He couldn't remember when a woman had roused him to such heights.

He parked the pickup in the driveway, got out and went into the house.

Toys littered the kitchen floor. An open package of cookies rested on the cabinet. In the living room, the television droned.

"Deannie?" Brodie called, his gaze sweeping the chaos. "Buster? Angel?"

When he received no answer, Brodie walked up the stairs. Where were they?

"Deannie?" he repeated, pushing open the door to the guest bedroom. Her duffel bag rested in the middle of her unmade bed, her socks rolled into a ball on the floor. The shirt he'd loaned her the night before lay folded neatly across the back of a chair.

Brodie moved on past to the bedroom that Angel and Buster had been sharing since Patsy Ann had left Kenny. What he saw had him smiling.

Deannie was sitting in the rocking chair, Angel and Buster cradled in her lap. All three were sound asleep, a picture book lay open in Deannie's lap.

An odd tenderness enveloped him at the scene. She looked for all the world like a true Madonna. So she couldn't keep house. She was good with the children and a sight better looking than Matilda.

Brodie didn't have the heart to wake her and tell her she was expected to cook lunch for six hungry ranch hands.

Instead he tiptoed downstairs, took the last of the roast beef from the refrigerator and began making sandwiches. Whistling to himself, Brodie realized he felt happier than he had in a very long time.

Chapter Four

Like shooting fish in a barrel, Deannie thought, slanting Brodie a glance. He was looking at her as if she were a delicious confection, his eyes bright and shining, the expression on his face one of moonstruck delight. She'd changed into skimpy denim shorts and a white halter top after lunch, hoping for this exact effect. If she had known winning him over would be this easy, she would never have bothered learning to play poker.

They were standing in the front yard appraising her vehicle while Buster and Angel fed sugar cubes to Brodie's horse, which was tied beside a weeping willow tree. The breeze rustled through the leaves, cooling Deannie's sun-baked skin.

"Rory couldn't find anything wrong with your car, but that doesn't mean it won't act up on you again," Brodie said. "He did say it needed lots of maintenance work. Oil change, fuel filter, spark plugs. When was the last time you had it serviced?"

Deannie shrugged. "I don't remember."

A smile curled his lips. "I know. It's not the sort of thing a lady generally worries about. Truthfully, Deannie, you need a man to look after you.''

Normally she would have bristled at such a remark, but coming from Brodie, it was perfect. He was playing right into her hands, perceiving her as a helpless female. Capturing his attention was far too effortless. The man was guileless and gullible. He believed everything she told him. Guilt plucked her conscience like a tightly strung violin. She was taking advantage of his good nature, using him to gain what she wanted more than anything else in the world.

Yes, wooing Brodie Trueblood was like shooting plentiful fish in a tiny barrel. But then again, how many times had her father uttered that same clichéd phrase when betting on a "sure thing" only to have his misbegotten wager blow up in his face?

Don't take anything for granted, Deanna Rene Hollis, she warned herself. *Never let your guard down.*

"Rory will take care of all that stuff for you while you're staying with us," Brodie was saying.

"Thank you," she said.

"You're welcome." His smile broadened to encompass his eyes.

"And thanks again for making lunch for the ranch hands." She reached out to touch his arm.

Her fingers sizzled at the contact. Brodie swallowed hard, and his Adam's apple bobbed.

"Hey, you needed the rest. Running after those two is a chore unto itself." Brodie jerked a thumb at the children.

Deannie peered over her shoulder. Buster was swinging on the horse's reins and Angel was tugging at his bottom lip. Ranger tolerated their antics with long-suffering patience.

"Oh, heavens," Deannie exclaimed and hustled across the short distance to apprehend the two little hoydens before they could do any more damage to the poor horse.

"Buster, stop that this minute. Angel, get your finger out of Ranger's mouth before he chomps it off."

Startled, Angel jerked her finger back and started to cry. Deannie squatted on the ground beside her and scooped the child into her lap. "What's wrong?"

"You yelleded at me." Angel's bottom lip protruded.

"I'm sorry, I didn't mean to yell, I was just scared Ranger was going to bite you," Deannie apologized. Were all kids this sensitive and this active?

"Yeah, stoopid, whatcha mean sticking your finger in the horse's mouth?" her brother taunted, placing his palms on his knees and wagging his head back and forth in front of his sister.

"I not stoopid," Angel declared, tears drying into salty streaks on her round cheeks. She jumped to her feet and knotted her tiny hands into fists. "I want to see if he ated the sugar."

Deannie looked over at Brodie. He had a hand clamped over his mouth, and his shoulders shook with mirth.

"You're a big help," she told him.

"Hey, they're not my kids." He pursed his lips, still struggling to contain his laughter.

His kids.

Why did the vivid image of a miniature Brodie and a small red-haired girl that looked just like herself, leap to mind? If she married this man, having his babies was a distinct possibility. And having his children meant making love.

Deannie's heart trilled at the idea of making love to Brodie Trueblood. Of course if she succeeded in getting him to marry her, they would most definitely have to have sex. There would be no avoiding physical intimacy with such a potent male.

She envisioned his arms wrapped around her, those full lips responding to hers with unbridled passion. At that moment she could almost taste him. Birth control would most certainly be in order. A man this sexy, this virile could get her pregnant simply by hanging his trousers next to hers. Nervously Deannie dropped her gaze, terrified he might read her errant thoughts.

The notion was a jolt from the blue. Having kids definitely was not part of the game plan. Children would make getting divorced that much harder.

Divorce.

Such an ugly word with disastrous repercussions for little ones. No. There would be no children from this union.

Deannie's mood plummeted. Why did she suddenly feel so sad? She'd never wanted children before. She would be getting what she'd ached to possess for the past fifteen years—Willow Creek. Nothing else mattered.

"Come on, Ranger, let's get you out of harm's way." Brodie rescued his horse from Buster. "Well, I best be getting back to work," he said, addressing Deannie. He pulled the brim of his hat down lower over his dark eyes. "We usually eat supper at six-thirty. Will that be a problem?"

Deannie shook her head. "No problem."

No problem? Who was she kidding? She needed a crash course in cooking. The only thing she knew how to prepare was macaroni and cheese from a box.

Brodie swung astride Ranger's back and gathered the reins in his hands. "See you then." Lifting his hand to his temple, he gave her a salute and trotted off across the field.

Deannie watched him go. He cut an impressive figure riding tall in the saddle, his broad shoulders swaying in practiced rhythm with his horse. Something caught in Deannie's throat. An emotion she couldn't name, and it fluttered there, unfettered by common sense.

Stop fantasizing about him, Deanna Hollis. There can't be a true romance between you two. Remember, no matter how attractive he might be, the man is still Rafe Trueblood's son and your sworn enemy.

* * *

She scrambled his brains.

Whenever he was around Deannie McCellan, Brodie could think of nothing else but kissing those enticing lips. When he'd witnessed her tending to the children he'd experienced a sudden fondness so overwhelming he knew he had to get away from her and pronto. The sensations whirling inside him, more powerful than a Texas-size twister, had him trembling in his boots. It was far too soon to be feeling the things he felt for this beautiful woman.

"You don't know anything about her, Trueblood," he spoke out loud as Ranger loped the back forty. He was scouting for a dozen Herefords that had gone astray from the herd. "For all you know she could be a scheming gold digger after your ranch."

It wouldn't be the first time he'd encountered a conniving female. In the weeks since Rafe's death, several of the local girls had set their caps for him, hoping to become the mistress of Willow Creek. Some had sent him coy looks in church, others had mailed him condolence letters along with invitations to parties and dances. A bold few had even come out to the ranch on the pretext of helping him deal with the grief over his father's demise. But none of those women had caught his interest. And despite his anxiousness to find a mate and get married, Brodie had seen through the girls and their calculated manipulations. It hadn't been difficult to pinpoint his sudden surge in popularity.

Was Deannie McCellan like that? Frowning, Brodie clicked his tongue and guided Ranger around a clump of cactus. He hated to believe that of her, but his cautious nature warned him to be careful. He hadn't turned Willow Creek into a thriving cattle ranch by taking unnecessary risks.

Still, he couldn't help how he felt about Deannie.

He had to find out more about her. Where she came from, what she hoped for from the future, her likes and dislikes.

No matter how attractive he might find the woman, they couldn't build a future together if she was a flighty party girl or a status-seeking social climber. He needed a real woman who wasn't afraid to roll up her sleeves and work by his side for common goals.

Determined to provide the upstanding solid stability he had not received as a child, Brodie required a mate who wanted the same things from life—a secure home, a loving family, a supportive community. He did not know if Deannie met these requirements. Before he started falling head-over-heels, he needed answers to his questions.

"I'll proceed with care." He nodded to himself. There was only one kink in his plan—as soon as Patsy Ann came home from the hospital Deannie McCellan would be leaving Willow Creek.

Brodie ran a hand along his jaw. What to do? He hated to let her get away. What if Deannie decided to disappear before they had a chance to explore this magnetic pull between them? Would he regret it for the rest of his life?

There was only one thing to do—offer her the housekeeper's job on a permanent basis. After all, with three children to chase and six ranch hands to feed, Patsy Ann would need all the help she could get.

Deannie had been on her way to a job interview when her car had broken down in Yarborough. Unless Santa Fe held some unknown attraction for her, there was a good chance she would take him up on the offer.

Satisfied he was doing the right thing in extending Deannie the position, Brodie spotted the wayward cattle and spurred the gelding into a canter.

"Mix one-half cup of milk with two cups of bread crumbs," Deannie read out loud from the cookbook spread open in front of her. Biting her tongue in concentration, she followed the instructions.

Flour handprints graced the front of her apron. Her hair,

which she'd pulled back into a ponytail before attempting this feat, had worked itself loose and was now trailing into her face. Deannie puffed out her cheeks and blew upward, trying to lift the escaping tendril out of her eyes, without having to stop and wash her hands.

Buster and Angel, being exceptionally cooperative for once, were still ensconced at the kitchen table where she'd left them with molding clay, aluminum cookie cutters and instructions to be very quiet while she prepared dinner.

Deannie poured the milk and bread crumbs into the concoction masquerading as a meat loaf and squished the mess with her hands. The action produced an unexpected memory, and she hissed in a deep breath at the onslaught.

Here, in this very kitchen, she remembered her mother kneading bread on this same counter. She could hear her mother's melodious voice as she hummed, "Down in the Valley." For a fleeting moment she could actually see her mother standing there, a welcome smile on her familiar face. Deannie's heart lurched. Her nose twitched. She knew it was all in her imagination, but a faint yeasty odor permeated the room.

"Oh, Mama," Deannie whispered under her breath, her chest tightening.

Any lingering doubts she might have been harboring concerning the rightness of her deception disappeared in that instant. Willow Creek belonged to her. The memories, so fresh and vivid, reassured her that this was indeed her home. Her mother had lived here. Had died right out there in the horse paddock, thrown from an unruly stallion.

Deannie gulped against the tide of emotions running through her. She'd been cheated of her birthright. Her past stolen, desecrated by those thieving Truebloods.

Except Brodie. He's different from Rafe and Kenny, the little voice in the back of her mind nudged.

She pushed that thought aside, clinging instead to her

anger. Anger she'd cultivated for so many years. Anger intensified by her father's recent suicide.

Deannie clenched her fists, and hamburger meat oozed between her fingers. Somebody had to pay for what she'd suffered. Too bad it had to be Brodie.

Squaring her shoulders, Deannie mentally renewed her resolve. She had to win Brodie's heart, and she had to do it quickly. She had until Patsy Ann came home from the hospital to convince him she was the woman of his dreams.

"You not suppose to eat it."

Buster's childish voice snapped Deannie from her reverie. Uh-oh, this didn't sound good. What were they up to?

"What are you kids doing?" she asked, standing on tiptoe to peer over the bar at the two imps in the dining room.

"She made a star," Buster explained. "But then she ate it."

"Angel!" Wiping her hands on her apron, Deannie darted around the corner to find Angel with a guilty expression and bits of blue clay sticking to her teeth.

"It didn't taste good." The child made a face.

Deannie froze, her pulse racing. She had no idea what one did in a situation like this. Call 911? Induce vomiting? Feed her bread?

She placed a palm under Angel's mouth. "Spit it out," Deannie commanded.

"Can't."

"Why not?"

"I swallowed it."

Deannie groaned. She'd have to tell Brodie right away, but where was he? He could be anywhere on the ranch. Terrified, she wrung her hands and struggled to get control of herself.

Think, Deannie, think.

As if in answer to her silent prayer, the back door opened and Brodie strolled inside.

"Thank God you're here!" Deannie breathed and rushed

over to clutch his arm. It felt so strong and reassuring in her grasp that she had to choke back a lump of gratitude.

"They were that bad, huh?" Brodie's brown eyes crinkled at the edges, teasing her.

"This is serious. Angel just ate some molding clay. We've got to do something!"

Brodie raised his palms. "Calm down, Deannie, you're talking a mile a minute and I can't understand a word you're saying."

Buster and Angel hovered nearby, eyes wide in terror. Lord, she'd frightened them, too. Stamping her foot in frustration, Deannie wiped at the tears welling in her eyes.

"Angel poisoned herself with clay and it's all my fault!"

"Do you mean this?" Brodie strode across the room to retrieve the box of clay from the table. He held it up for her to examine. In bright red letters the box read "nontoxic."

"Oh."

Feeling like a monumental fool, Deannie dropped her gaze and studied the floor intently.

"Don't worry, honey." Brodie chuckled. "Angel will be just fine."

Honey.

That simple word created a knot of anxiety inside her. Could it be guilt galloping over her spine? But she had nothing to feel guilty about, the Truebloods were the ones with blood on their hands, not her.

"I'm sorry I got excited over nothing," Deannie apologized. "Trouble is, I'm not used to kids."

"Couldn't tell it by me," Brodie said, scooping Angel into his arms and wiping the clay from her face. "You're wonderful with them. And I'd rather have you worried unnecessarily than being lackadaisical about their welfare like Matilda was."

"I should have kept a closer eye on them," Deannie fretted. "But it was time to start supper, and I had to keep them occupied somehow. I never dreamed they'd *eat* the clay.''

''I didn't eat it,'' Buster said, thrusting out his chest proudly.

''I sorry,'' Angel wailed. ''I didn't mean to.''

''Oh, sweetie.'' Deannie moved to where Brodie stood holding her and grasped Angel's little foot in her hand. ''It's not your fault.''

Brodie gave Deannie the once-over. She could just imagine how she appeared. Flour on her face, hair in disarray, apron askew. Flustered, Deannie pushed her hair from her face and retied her bedraggled apron strings.

''Looks like they've run you through the wringer,'' Brodie noted. ''Tell you what, I'll take these two terrors off your hands while you concentrate on fixing supper.''

''Would you?''

She hadn't intended on sounding so desperate. She'd wanted to prove to Brodie that she could handle the children, cook dinner and clean the house, but she'd failed miserably. Without any wifely skills under her belt how did she hope to coax him into marriage? He might find her attractive, yes, but she knew he would be looking for the type of woman who could help him run Willow Creek. With her current track record, she was lucky he hadn't asked her to pack her bags and get out.

''Unc' Brodie,'' Buster whined, hopping from foot to foot, obviously jealous of his younger sister's place in Brodie's arms. ''I wanna piggyback ride.''

''Hold on, partner. Let me bend down, and you crawl on.''

''Yeah!'' Buster said and placed a booted foot squarely in Brodie's back.

Brodie groaned then struggled to a standing position, Buster's arms wrapped tightly around his neck.

''You look like a pack horse.'' Deannie giggled.

''I feel like one.''

"I don't know how single parents survive," she said. "Especially with more than one child."

"Neither do I." Brodie shook his head. "But in some cases I think a single-family household is better than one in which a parent sets a poor example."

His eyes met Deannie's. His mouth was drawn down in a firm, hard line, and she wondered if he was thinking about Rafe. She knew what it was like to be disappointed with a father. She and Brodie Trueblood had far more in common than Deannie cared to admit.

"I was about to go help Cooter feed the calves, you two monkeys want to come?" Brodie addressed the kids.

"Yeah!" they hollered in unison.

Cooter? Cooter Gates? Deannie's blood turned to ice at the mention of the foreman's name. When she'd orchestrated this charade it had never occurred to her that Cooter Gates would still be working at Willow Creek. Not after fifteen years. Not with the change in ownership.

What was she going to do? She'd only been seven years old when Cooter had last seen her, but how many redhaired Deannies had he met in the course of his lifetime? He was bound to put two and two together the minute he saw her and learned her name.

Fear swamped her. She'd couldn't fail. Not now. Not yet. Not without a fight. She'd waited too long for the day when she would be old enough, brave enough and accomplished enough to achieve her goal. She must concoct a way out of this.

Cooter Gates had the power to send her scheme crashing down around her ears. One word from him and she would never have the chance to convince Brodie to fall in love with her, and she would never reclaim the family homestead.

She had to avoid Cooter, that's all there was to it. But how?

"Deannie?" Brodie's voice cut through her panic.

She jerked her head up. Her pulse thudded furiously in the hollow of her neck.

"We'll be back in about an hour."

"Uh. Okay."

The screen door snapped shut behind them, the children's high-pitched giggles still echoing in the silent kitchen.

Like a gambler holding a pair of deuces, whose bluff has been called, Deannie returned to the meat loaf with a heavy heart. Defeat was imminent unless she did something fast.

Throwing the meat loaf into the oven, she quickly peeled potatoes and set them on to boil. She opened a large can of green beans, dumped them into a pan then slapped them on the stove to warm. Head down, hands clasped behind her back, she paced the tiled floor.

There's got to be a solution.

But instead of imagining a way out of her dilemma, she kept seeing Brodie's face. Cringing, she envisioned how he would look when Cooter Gates recognized her and revealed who she really was. She saw Brodie's mouth harden into the same unforgiving expression he'd turned on Kenny the evening before. Deannie shuddered. Her chance to live at Willow Creek Ranch again could forever be shattered by one sentence from the old foreman.

Perhaps if she hid her hair. Tied it up in a scarf. It would buy her some time until she could come up with a permanent answer.

Grasping at straws, Deannie left the food cooking and scurried upstairs to her bedroom. She braided her hair and coiled it around her head. Pinning it into place, she covered the whole thing with a blue bandanna.

She looked at her reflection in the mirror and laughed. Well, if Brodie Trueblood was looking for a rancher's wife, he need search no farther. Staring back at her was the epitome of a country girl. Fresh-faced with no makeup, apron stained with food, hair covered in a work scarf, nobody would mistake Deannie McCellan for a glamour queen or even a bar dolly, for that matter.

Please, let this work, she sent a prayer to the heavens, then hurried back downstairs just in time to rescue supper.

This was her plan. She'd set the table, lay out the food then disappear upstairs when the ranch hands came stomping through the door. If Cooter caught sight of her, maybe he wouldn't think twice about her identity. She expected Brodie to come check on her but she had that covered. She'd tell him she had a headache.

Another fib.

Getting honorable now, Deannie? her conscience gnawed. Dang. It was Brodie Trueblood's fault. If he had been like his father and brother, she would have no qualms about taking Willow Creek away from him.

But he's not like them, is he?

No. He wasn't. Brodie was kind and generous, honest and true. But was she so wrong, hoping to get him to marry her? After all, she was attracted to him and he to her or so it seemed. What was so bad about marrying to obtain something? People did it all the time.

But not under false pretenses.

Deannie pressed her hands over her ears in a vain attempt to drown out her nagging inner voices and didn't hear the footsteps on the back porch until it was too late to flee.

Impending doom seized her. Ominous strains of the funeral march resounded in her head. At any moment the jig could be up, and Deannie would find herself tossed out onto the road. Trembling, she pressed her palms together and watched the back door swing open.

"Deannie?"

Brodie. His boot heels scraped against the cement steps. Her heart pounded in response.

"Yes?" She twisted her fingers into a knot behind her back and held her breath.

"Hi." He grinned, stepping into the room. "Something smells delicious."

"Where are the kids?" she asked. "I'll feed them in the kitchen."

"Rory's got them. They're right behind me." Brodie's eyes narrowed as he came closer. "Are you all right? You look funny."

"S-s-sure," she stammered. Heck, she didn't need Cooter to give her away, she was doing a damned fine job of it herself. "Why?"

"Your face is flushed. Like you have a fever."

Before she could move, before she could react, he reached over and laid his palm across her forehead.

That simple act sent blood surging through her veins in quick, vicious spurts. She suddenly felt light-headed. Reaching out, she grasped the back of a chair and curled her fingers around it for support.

"Just hot in the kitchen."

"Is that why you tied your hair up?"

"Uh-huh." Why didn't he take his hand away!

"I guess that's it. You don't feel like you have a fever." Almost reluctantly he dropped his arm to his side, and Deannie breathed a sigh of relief.

"I'm fine."

"That's good. I'd hate for you to get sick."

His tenderness was a stake through her chest. It's only because he needs you to watch after the kids, she told herself. That's all.

From outside she heard the others treading up the porch steps.

"Here come the troops," Brodie said. "You missed them at lunch but now you'll have a chance to meet everybody."

That's exactly what she was afraid of.

"Now that you mention it," Deannie said, fingering her brow. "I do feel a sick headache coming on."

Concern etched his features, and aggravated compunction gnawed a gaping chasm in her soul.

"I'll get you some aspirin," he offered.

But it was too late. The ranch hands poured through the door, Angel and Buster riding the shoulders of two men.

Deannie saw Cooter Gates and she inhaled sharply, waiting for his cry of accusation.

The foreman walked slowly, his hands moving before him to feel the way. Blinking, Deannie shook her head. She had recalled him as an old man, but that had been from a child's point of view. He was probably in his early sixties, she estimated, still slim, wearing the same Western-style plaid shirts she remembered. His hair was grayer, and he sported a scraggly beard, but what captured her attention were his eyes.

Eyes that had once been blue and lively with a teasing light were now vacant and icy.

Eyes ruined by too many days spent in the hot Texas sun without protective sunglasses.

Eyes scarred white by cataracts.

One ranch hand offered his arm, and Cooter took it for support as he maneuvered into the dining room.

Realization struck Deannie hard. Sadness mingled with relief as she watched the older man settle into his chair.

Cooter was blind. He couldn't recognize her.

She was saved. Deannie took the old man's blindness as a clear, unmistakable sign. The heavens were in agreement. She was indeed the rightful owner of Willow Creek Ranch.

Chapter Five

What was the matter with Deannie? She was acting mighty skittish this evening. Had that incident with Angel eating the clay affected her so strongly?

Brodie slid a glance her way, but she hadn't spoken a word since supper. Those two preschoolers could definitely produce stress. Perhaps it was just a headache that plagued her, but he felt uneasy. When he'd introduced her to Cooter, and the old foreman had commented on her name, Deannie's unusual reaction hadn't been imaginary. She'd gripped the table with both hands until her knuckles turned white, and she'd held her breath for the longest time.

What was it Cooter had said? Something about once having known a little girl named Deannie. Why would that upset her? Puzzled, Brodie scratched his head.

Deannie washed dishes at the sink. Metal utensils clanked against stainless steel. Her sleeves were rolled up past her elbows, and she seemed studiously intent on scrubbing the floral pattern off his mother's plates.

Thankfully, she had changed from that skimpy little halter top and those thigh-high denim shorts into jeans and a long-sleeved cotton shirt. That provocative outfit had given his libido a run for his money. Brodie hated to admit it, but he admired the casual way she could go from sexy siren to fresh-faced country girl at the drop of a hat.

Yes, Deannie McCellan was something special. That's why he wanted to find out what was bothering her. He hoped her first day on the job hadn't been too much for her or that she was considering quitting before he had a chance to offer her the position on a permanent basis.

The ranch hands were in the living room watching television with Buster and Angel. Brodie finished clearing the table and brought the remaining dishes over to the sink.

His gaze trailed down Deannie's back and lingered on that well-toned tush encased so enticingly in those blue jeans. Even with her hair tied up she was gorgeous. Brodie had a sudden urge to peel that bandana from her head, tug the pins from her hair and let it float free and silky over his fingers. Everything about her pushed his buttons.

"If you'll put Buster and Angel to bed, I'll finish washing the dishes," he offered.

Deannie turned to look at him. Her blue eyes, muted in the fluorescent lighting, appeared a little sad. "It's a deal."

"How's your headache?"

"Better."

"Maybe you'd like to come sit out on the porch with me when you get the kids down."

"Maybe."

Her expression remained noncommittal, her tone even and devoid of emotion. He couldn't read her. What was she thinking?

"It's a nice night."

She nodded.

"There's banana nut ice cream in the freezer. We could enjoy a bowl and watch the fireflies flicker through the honeysuckle," he tempted.

"Maybe," she repeated.

"I'd like to speak to you about something important. Please meet me on the porch in forty-five minutes," he said, refusing to take "maybe" for an answer.

"All right," she said at last, and Brodie felt as if he'd just won a coveted prize.

She departed upstairs with the children in tow, and Brodie turned his attention to the dishes. It was nice having Deannie around the house, he admitted. All day he'd looked forward to coming home and getting to know her better.

Brodie whistled tunelessly. The supper hadn't been too bad. The meat loaf had been a little dry and the potatoes lumpy but hungry ranch hands seldom noticed such things. Besides, the clay-eating crisis had probably affected supper's outcome. With practice, Deannie would be a damned fine cook.

He prayed Buster and Angel would be so tired they'd fall asleep as soon as their heads hit the pillow. He wanted Deannie McCellan with him, on the front porch swing, looking up at the stars and telling him all about herself.

The television clicked off, and the ranch hands shuffled through the kitchen, Rory guiding Cooter around the furniture. They wished Brodie good-night and soon disappeared out the back door.

Thankful silence ensued.

Brodie wiped down the countertop, then checked his watch. Ten minutes until the rendezvous.

Feeling more nervous than Rafe Trueblood at an old-fashioned tent revival prayer meeting, Brodie paced the kitchen. He struggled to tamp down his almost overwhelming desire for Deannie McCellan. It wasn't good to be so anxious. This inexplicable magnetism drawing Brodie to her could lead him into grave trouble if he wasn't careful. Before he surrendered his heart, before he started dreaming of a future with this woman, he simply had to know more about her.

Beginning now.

The stairs creaked, and his pulse skipped. Swallowing hard, Brodie retrieved the ice cream from the freezer in the corner and busied himself scooping it into bowls. Without looking up, he heard her enter the kitchen on kitten-quiet feet.

"Kids down for the count?" he asked, arranging his lips in a pleasant but distant smile. He must not let her see how much she affected him. Not yet. Maintain a poker face. He'd never been a card player but he knew the basics. He was, after all, Rafe's son. Never tip your hand until you know you can win.

Deannie nodded. "It only took four pages of *Curious George*."

"They had fun today," Brodie commented. "I haven't seen them laugh this much since Patsy Ann left Kenny and moved in here. It's been tough on them."

"Family problems usually are."

Something flickered in her eyes. Something dark. Something disturbing. Something hidden deep inside her. Was she speaking from personal experience. Had she grown up in a broken home or worse?

"They like you," Brodie said, handing Deannie the heaping bowls and pushing aside his morbid thoughts.

She'd taken her hair down, he noticed, attempting to ignore his body's instant response to the lovely sight. Turning, he stowed the ice cream carton back in the freezer compartment. "When I took them outside to feed the calves they chattered nonstop about you."

"I like them, too." A Mona Lisa smile lifted her mouth. "It's funny. I've never been around small children, and I thought I wouldn't enjoy it much, but I do."

"They can be a handful, no doubt about it." Brodie reached over and placed his hand lightly on Deannie's elbow. "But they are great."

To his delight she didn't pull back. Instead, she allowed

him to guide her down the hallway and out onto the front porch.

"We'll leave the door open," he said. "In case the kids wake up and call for us."

"You act like their father."

Brodie frowned. "That's because their own father won't assume his parental responsibilities." Thinking of his brother sent a spark of anger flaring though him. "But let's not ruin the moment by talking about Kenny. I just want to sit here and enjoy my ice cream."

The porch swing creaked as they settled into it together. The dish of ice cream burned cold in his hands.

A slight breeze blew, tousling Deannie's flame red mane. Cicadas buzzed in the mimosa tree on the front lawn. Buster's tricycle sat overturned on the sidewalk. The large climbing yellow rosebush his mother had planted fifteen years ago was in full bloom, crawling all over the white lattice trellis. The sweet aroma drifted over to them.

Brodie remembered when they had planted that bush. He and Mama together. His mother had been so proud to finally have a permanent place to call her own. And not just a humble home but a fine farmhouse. Overnight she'd gone from a shanty hovel to Willow Creek Ranch.

He knew his mother had always felt guilty about the way Rafe had obtained the ranch, but she'd been so excited over their own good fortune, she had pushed thoughts of that other family aside. After all, she'd stuck by her husband through the bad times, and Melinda Trueblood considered the ranch her reward for long-suffering service. But she'd been unable to shake her own culpability.

Looking out across the yard, Brodie wondered what had happened to Gil Hollis and his little daughter. She'd be grown by now, he realized. In her early twenties. Now that Rafe was gone maybe he could track her down, find some way to make amends for what had happened. He imagined she held no love for the Truebloods.

Shaking his head to dispel the remorse that gnawed at him anytime he thought about Gil Hollis, Brodie turned his attention to the dazzling woman at his side.

Deannie, too, was surveying the land around them. She sat up straight, her posture rigid, a faraway expression in her eyes as if she were viewing something from the past. Again, he got the strangest sensation that she was hiding something.

"You've got a beautiful place here, Brodie Trueblood."

"Thank you. It's my pride and joy. When my father…er…bought it." He hesitated over the words. No point telling Deannie the sordid truth about his old man. At least not yet. "The previous owner had a drinking problem and had allowed the place to fall into ruins."

"And your father fixed it up."

There was no denying the sarcasm in her voice. Startled, Brodie studied her face. Had she heard about Rafe? What had Kenny divulged to her during that card game?

"No," Brodie replied, his tone harsh. "I'm the one who made Willow Creek into the thriving spread it is today."

"You must be very proud."

"I've worked hard for everything I've achieved."

"I'll bet." Deannie clenched her jaw. Was that anger he'd seen flit across her forehead? Why would she be mad? Did she come from a poverty-stricken environment? Did she resent people who'd made something of themselves? What was her story? His curiosity was almost as strong as his physical desire for her.

"Your ice cream is melting," she commented, pointing a finger at his bowl.

"Oh." Brodie took a bite of the sweet treat. Never had bananas tasted so fresh, so sharp against his tongue. Was it his heightened awareness of Deannie McCellan that brought everything more into focus?

She peeked over at him. He could smell her sweet magnolia scent. Her aroma mingled with the taste of ice cream and increased his level of arousal. It had been a very long time since anyone had so commanded his attention, and Brodie wasn't sure what to do about his desire, except try his best to suppress it. But it would be damned hard with her sitting beside him, looking so kissable.

"My father died a little over two weeks ago," Brodie explained. "I guess I haven't really come to grips with his death yet."

She clicked her tongue. "I know how hard it is."

"My father and I weren't very close. But in an odd way, that makes it harder to accept. Now I'll never be able to tell him that I did love him in spite of everything that happened between us."

"That's a shame."

"What about your father?"

"My father's dead, too. He passed away six months ago, and we were very close." She stirred her spoon in the melted ice cream.

"So you do understand."

"Yes."

"You feel unsettled, disjointed, out of place. Like nothing that used to be important matters anymore. You start looking for answers to impossible questions, like What's the meaning of life? and Why am I here? It's disconcerting."

"Exactly." She knew how he felt. That empathy strengthened their connection.

Deannie shrugged. "That's the reason I was headed for New Mexico. I'm looking for a fresh start. There's nothing to keep me in Texas."

"Nothing?"

She shook her head.

Me. Brodie thought. *Am I reason enough to stay?*

"Actually," he said, "I wanted to talk to you about your trip to New Mexico."

"Oh?" She looked at him with her steady blue-eyed gaze.

Suddenly the air left Brodie's body as surely as if he had been thrown from the back of his horse. Why did a single glance from this woman send him into turmoil?

"Yeah," he continued once he'd managed to inhale again. "I've been thinking, even after Patsy Ann gets back home, we're still going to need someone around to do the cooking and cleaning."

"What are you saying?" Deannie pursed those peachy lips, and Brodie just about choked on his ice cream.

"I'm offering you the housekeeper job on a permanent basis. That is if you're interested."

She didn't answer right away.

"It pays five-hundred a month plus room and board," he wheedled. Lord, why did he ache so badly for her to say yes?

"I don't know."

"Do you have a man waiting for you in Santa Fe?"

Damn! Why had he asked that question? Brodie set his empty bowl down on the porch and avoided her gaze. He waited, breath bated, for her response.

"No."

"Family there?"

"I have no family."

His heart tripped. There was no reason for her not to stay. Excitement jabbed his gut. "Uh...I've got another reason for hoping you'll take this job."

"You do?" One orange-red eyebrow arched prettily.

Brodie shifted and moved closer toward her. He rested his arm on the back of the swing. His boots scraped against the porch and the swing's chain squeaked its protest.

"I like you, Deannie." His voice was gruffer than he intended, smoky from the heated emotions burning his chest.

"I like you too, Brodie."

Her smile was genuine, honest and filled him to the bursting point with joy.

"Don't get me wrong," he hastened to add, fearful that she might read an ulterior motive into his job offer. He didn't want her believing he was conspiring to take advantage of her. "This is strictly a business arrangement. I want you to know that I don't have hanky-panky on my mind."

"You don't?" Her tone was rich, cool as silk.

"No, ma'am." He ran a hand through his hair.

"Why not?"

Her question surprised him so much that Brodie almost toppled off the porch swing. Here's where he needed to tiptoe prudently. Before he got more deeply involved with Deannie McCellan he must first discover whether she was interested in Brodie Trueblood, the person, or Brodie Trueblood, the successful rancher.

"Because I respect you."

She eyed him. "You're not pulling my leg are you?"

"Absolutely not," he swore.

"You're a breed all your own, Brodie Trueblood."

"I'm probably not like the kind of men you're used to."

"No," she said, "you're not. But I'm glad for that."

It was time to tell her what was on his mind. He'd be up front with his feelings. Brodie didn't believe in playing mind games or toying with someone's affections.

"Truth is, Deannie, I want to get to know you better, but I need to take things slowly. There's a lot going on in my life—settling my father's estate, getting used to having Patsy Ann and her three kids living in the house, dealing with my brother, Kenny, keeping the ranch on track. I currently don't have much time for myself, but I will eventually. How do you feel about that?"

"Let me see if I understand you correctly." Deannie tucked a strand of hair behind her ear. "You're seeking a totally professional relationship between us, but you think you might, at some point in the future, be interested in changing the nature of that relationship.''

Her blue eyes glistened in the moonlight, and Brodie felt as if he could see right into her soul. Her pupils widened as their stare continued. An odd sensation grabbed him with an urgency he didn't understand. This link between them seemed to transcend time and place. To carry them beyond the mundane and up into the stars.

He'd never been one to believe in reincarnation and past lives and all that other New Age stuff, but if such things were true, Brodie would swear he'd known Deannie McCellan in another existence. The invisible cord binding them was that strong.

"That's correct." He mumbled, barely able to speak.

"Before I accept your offer, there's one thing I need to know."

"Yes?"

"Does this mean that you couldn't kiss me?"

Warning, danger, proceed at your own risk! Take it easy, Trueblood.

"Do you want me to kiss you?"

In answer, she allowed her eyes to drift closed, and she tilted her chin up to him.

Should he kiss her? Was it smart?

Brodie clenched his jaw, his mind at war with his physical body. He wanted to taste her. So much it caused a searing ache deep down in his lower abdomen.

"Brodie," she cooed, soft as the evening breeze raising the hairs on his wrists.

Stifling a groan, he succumbed to temptation and closed the small gap between them. The swing rocked back and forth as he gathered her into his arms.

He pressed his face against the top of her head. Her hair smelled of magnolia flowers and warm sunshine. He felt her heart beating against her slender rib cage, tapping out a frantic flurry. She wanted him. Whether the desire was purely physical or something more he couldn't tell, but he did know she was not faking her response.

Her whole body trembled. Her back arched, and she pushed her chest hungrily against his. Tossing her head, she whimpered and exposed her long neck to him.

Brodie took the invitation for what it was and lowered his mouth to cover an enticing patch of her peaches-and-cream complexion. Deannie melted at his touch, going limp in his arms as his tongue explored her vulnerable throat.

Like an out-of-control brushfire, sexual need leaped through him, chaotic and destructive. It had been years since he'd been with a woman and never one as sexy as Deannie McCellan.

He knew he should stop, put an end to this before he did something he might regret. But he couldn't. Not yet. Not without a taste of those beguiling lips.

Brodie wanted her. Here. Now. This minute and no amount of self-coaxing and cajoling could stop him.

"Deannie," he whispered and took her mouth with determination. Something about her caused the lurking savage in him to resurrect, making Brodie act in ways he had never before behaved.

Their kiss flared like a match touched to gasoline. She was the candle, and he the wick.

His forcefulness did not frighten her. She drank him in, her lips soft, cool and tasting of banana ice cream.

Her teeth parted, allowing him entry.

Brodie's tongue darted inside the moist recesses of her mouth, and a thrill shot clean through his bones. He felt free, unrestrained, wild. It was an incredible sensation, similar to busting an unruly stallion.

For too long he'd kept a damper on his emotions, tamping down his anger to please his mother. Biting his tongue when he longed to tell his father what he thought of him and his itinerant lifestyle. Such restraint had led him to hold back in other areas of his life.

Like romance.

In reality, he'd always been a little afraid of losing himself in a loving relationship. He'd seen firsthand what blind love had done to his mother and Patsy Ann. They'd both loved Trueblood men and it had gotten them nothing but heartache. Although he longed for a woman to offer him that kind of devotion, he was also terrified that he would end up with a female version of Rafe. A girl who liked to party and play cards and hang out in bars.

A girl like Deannie McCellan.

That sobering thought splashed over him, ice-water cold and just as startling. It was true, he'd first met her in a bar, drinking a beer and playing cards with Kenny and his friends. And now she was here, kissing him, a virtual stranger, with untamed abandon. How could he trust such a woman?

But what about the sweet girl who had cared so tenderly for Angel and Buster, the hopeful voice in the back of his head urged. Would someone who was just out for a good time treat those kids so kindly?

Maybe her concern for the children was all a carefully orchestrated act designed to win him over.

Suddenly Brodie felt as if he'd made a terrible mistake. Which was the real Deannie McCellan? A female goodtime Charlie or the devoted Madonna? What true nature lurked beneath that pretty face. Only time would tell. Until he knew for sure, he could not trust her.

"Brodie?"

He blinked, realizing he had stopped kissing her and pulled away.

"What's wrong?" She sat up and touched his shoulder.

Brodie suppressed a quiver and closed his eyes briefly, trying hard to fight off his consuming passion.

"I'm sorry," he said. "I didn't mean for this to go so far."

"Does the job offer still stand?"

He avoided looking at her. One glance into those blue eyes and he'd be lost again. "Yeah," he said. "But I think we'd better forgo the kissing for a while."

She nodded. "I agree."

Brodie got to his feet and walked to the edge of the porch. He had to remove himself from her immediate proximity or face the dire consequences of gathering her into his arms again.

Take a deep breath, Trueblood, and cool down.

He sucked in the sweet spring air, slipped his hands into his back pockets and stared out across the land.

The land that meant so much to him. The land he'd pampered and cultivated into the thriving outfit it was today. The land that suddenly seemed empty and worthless without somebody to share the future with him. He desperately needed a companion, a helpmate, a wife.

Could Deannie possibly be that woman?

"Brodie?"

The porch swing creaked, and he felt her come up behind him. He half turned and peered at her over his shoulder.

"I think we can make this work."

"What do you mean?"

"I confess I need a job and I'm very much attracted to you. But I'm also leery of getting involved with anyone. I've been hurt in the past, and I want to take things as slowly as you do."

There! Would a gold-digging female want to take things slowly? No. If she were after his money, she'd already be calling the preacher and ordering the dress.

"What are you saying, Deannie McCellan?" he asked, his tone low and throaty even to his own ears. Could she guess at the embers smoldering in his abdomen, at the stark desire eating a hole through him?

"I'm saying I would be honored to accept the position as your housekeeper for the period of three months. If, in that time, you'd like to renegotiate the conditions of my employment, then and only then will we explore the more personal nature of this relationship. Is it a deal?''

Deannie thrust her small hand toward him, an intent expression highlighting her delicate features.

"Deal." They shook on it.

She was murmuring all the right words, pushing all the right buttons, stoking the heat under his hopes and dreams. He had to be very careful, because Brodie knew one thing for sure.

Deannie McCellan had his heartstrings clutched firmly in a downward tug and she was yanking with all her might.

Brodie had played right into her plans.

She knew he'd been aching to get close to her. She'd seen desire masked in his dark eyes, read the intense longing in his body language. Then, after that earth-shattering kiss, when it seemed he might fold his hand in fear and retract the job offer, she'd quickly backed off, letting him think she wanted to take things as slowly as he did.

Too bad the man didn't indulge in poker, she could win back Willow Creek from him in one game. Deannie slid her eyes up and down Brodie's lean, muscular form. Now, if the man played strip poker that would be a whole other story.

The image of enacting strip poker with this ruggedly handsome man sent a heated flush rushing up her neck.

Deannie took her palm, the one that Brodie had just shaken, the one that still burned from his touch, and pressed it against her thigh. She wanted him to offer her marriage, yes. Her sole intent was to win Willow Creek, whatever the cost. But she did not wish to become so enamored of him that she lost her head. For no matter how different he seemed on the surface, Brodie was still Rafe Trueblood's son, and the acorn never fell far from the tree.

Trouble was, Brodie's explosive kiss had stirred her own desires. Desires she'd suppressed in favor of revenge. Desires she'd always denied, had never investigated, for fear she would lose her drive to regain the ranch. Suddenly she was faced with corralling intense longings, and she wasn't sure how to go about it.

This is stupid, Deannie. If your plan is going to work you can't allow your feelings to get out of control. Remember, no matter how attractive he is, Brodie's a Trueblood and no friend of yours.

Recalling what Brodie had said earlier about Gil Hollis not living up to his responsibilities and letting Willow Creek fall to ruin aroused Deannie's ire and cooled her ardor. Brodie had lied, as well, telling her Rafe had purchased the ranch, when in reality his old man had stolen the property from her father. Deannie had to remember his cavalier attitude. It would serve her well in the tough times ahead when she divorced Brodie and took him to court to fight for what was rightfully hers. For now, however, she had to concentrate on capturing his heart. Later, she would worry about ending the marriage.

High-beam headlights shone down the graveled road in front of the house as a vehicle rounded the corner.

"Looks like we got company," Brodie said.

A pickup truck with a loud muffler chugged into the drive. Brodie's face dissolved into a frown.

"Who is it?" Deannie asked.

"Kenny." Brodie practically spat his brother's name.

A sudden knot of fear twisted Deannie's stomach. How much had she revealed to Kenny during the course of their card game? Would he tell Brodie she'd tried to get him to wager the ranch? What would she do if Kenny voiced his knowledge to his brother?

Nervously, Deannie shifted her weight, racking her brains for a plausible explanation in case Kenny confronted her.

The truck door slammed, echoing loudly into the night.

Kenny, obviously intoxicated, weaved a path over to the front porch.

"Hey, li'l brother," he slurred.

"What are you doing here?" Brodie asked coldly.

Kenny hiccoughed and lurched backward, thrown off balance by the spasm. "I come to see my kids."

"You're drunk." Brodie folded his arms across his chest and widened his stance.

"Yeah? You wanna make something out of it?" Kenny doubled up his fists.

"I've had enough of fighting drunkards."

"Chicken." Kenny swayed on his feet. "The old man was right, you're nothing but a coward."

Standing behind him like she was, Deannie could almost feel Brodie's anger. He clenched his hands into fists and inhaled sharply. It was evident in his mannerisms that the old hurt ran deep and that the conflict between the two of them was nothing new. Deannie understood Brodie's contempt for his older brother. Her own father had disappointed her in countless ways. Chief among them, his suicide and losing Willow Creek.

"Go sleep it off in the barn," Brodie said.

"I come to see my kids, dammit."

"You can see them tomorrow."

"Get out of my way." Swinging his arms, Kenny started up the porch.

Brodie moved to block him. "It's ten o'clock. They've been in bed for over an hour."

Kenny looked surprised as if he had no idea of the time. "Well, wake them up."

"I will not. Those kids don't need to see you like this."

"Like what?"

"Reeking of cheap whiskey. You remind me so much of Rafe it's sickening."

"Don't you talk to me like that, you little snot." Kenny ducked his head and charged Brodie.

Deannie squealed and slapped a hand over her mouth. She had witnessed more than her share of these kinds of altercations, and they only ended in one way—somebody getting beat up. But it would be to her advantage if the two brothers remained angry with each other. A fight would cement their differences of opinions and keep Kenny from blabbing to Brodie about that card game at the Lonesome Dove.

Brodie sidestepped and Kenny crashed into the porch swing.

Bellowing like a bull who'd missed the matador, Kenny turned and dove at Brodie again.

Calmly, Brodie wadded up his fist and punched Kenny squarely on the jaw. Crumpling like cellophane, Kenny sank to the porch.

"I've never seen you this bad, big brother. What's happened to you?" Brodie asked, squatting down beside Kenny.

Despite the harshness in his voice, Deannie could tell Brodie still cared about his sibling. Just as she had loved her father in spite of his many failings.

Deannie couldn't help wondering how different things might have been if her mother hadn't died. Daddy probably wouldn't have turned to drink, and he would never have lost Willow Creek. She would have been raised in the lap of luxury surrounded by adoring parents and lots of friends. She would have been invited to the prom and gone to college.

Instead, she'd spent most of her childhood in shacks and bars. She'd suffered cruel taunts at school and endured her father's drinking binges. She'd never had a boyfriend, nor even many friends for that matter. Her higher education had come from the school of hard knocks. And learning to play poker in order to win back Willow Creek had become an all-consuming passion.

Deannie stood in the shadows, watching the drama between the two brothers unfold. Even though she was an outsider, she had a vested interest in the outcome. If the Trueblood men made peace with each other, she stood a good chance of having Kenny expose her as a conniving schemer just when she was trying to convince Brodie otherwise.

"What in the hell is wrong with you?" Brodie asked his brother.

"Patsy Ann," Kenny said with a strangled cry. Grunting, he maneuvered himself into a sitting position. "I went to see her at the hospital this evening."

"Did you go up there in this disgusting condition?" Brodie sounded horrified.

"No!" Kenny snapped. "For your information I spent the day looking for a job."

"So what's this all about?" Brodie waved a hand at his brother. "Why do you smell like you drank the whole brewery?"

"Patsy Ann told me tonight that she wants a divorce."

"Can you blame her?"

"When she walked out on me two weeks ago, I thought she was bluffing. That being nine months pregnant and hormonal had put her in a snit. Especially when she came to stay with you. I asked myself how mad could she be if she chose Willow Creek instead of going back home to her parents in Midland."

"You've pushed her to the limit."

Maudlin tears misted Kenny's eyes. "She looked so pretty sitting up in the hospital bed wearing that pink bed jacket I bought her when she had Angel. Patsy Ann's always looked gorgeous in pink. She was feeding the baby when I came in, but she wouldn't even glance my way."

"You've put her through a lot, Kenny. A woman can only take so much." Brodie extended his hand and tugged his brother to his feet.

"Mama never divorced the old man."

"Is that your excuse? The old man acted like a creep, and Mama kept taking it, so you thought you'd try it on Patsy Ann?"

Kenny's bottom lip trembled. "I love her, Brodie."

"You got a damned funny way of showing it."

"Well, everyone of us can't be Mr. Holier-Than-Thou like you," Kenny snarled. "This is all your fault."

"How do you figure that?" Brodie sank his hands on his hips and glared at his older brother.

Deannie stepped away and pressed her back against the cool wood of the farmhouse. Neither of them seemed to notice her. She knew firsthand the pain they were both experiencing, but she did not want to empathize with the Truebloods. She couldn't afford to care about them. She had to feed her anger in order to proceed with her strategy.

"If Rafe hadn't deeded you the ranch in his will, Patsy Ann would never have left me," Kenny accused.

"I didn't ask Rafe to leave the whole thing to me. I was as surprised by the inheritance as you were. In fact, it would have been just like him to shut me out completely."

"That's not true. The old man was damned proud of what you did with this ranch. Why else do you think he left it to you? He knew I'd lose it the same way he took it."

Brodie snorted and turned his head. Deannie saw from his expression that he was fighting some intense emotions. Was it disbelief mixing with the tentative hope that Kenny's words were true?

"I'm a screw-up," Kenny said glumly. "I've lost the best thing I've ever had." Tears slipped down his face.

Moving across the porch to cover the short distance between them, Brodie laid a comforting arm across Kenny's shoulder. "I can help you," he said. "Dammit, Kenny, I *want* to help you. I'd hate to see you drink yourself to death at fifty-five the way the old man did."

Kenny clung to his brother. "Would you do that for me?"

"You bet. But you've got to do exactly as I say."

Admiration for Brodie Trueblood blossomed in Deannie's chest. He was willing to assist his brother despite the problems of the past. But that admiration brought trepidation. If he and Kenny mended fences, what would it mean for Deannie? In a bid to protect Brodie, would Kenny tell him what he knew about her? She twisted her fingers into knots and held her breath. Perhaps once Kenny was sober she could have a long talk with him.

"I'll try," Kenny said, clasping the hand Brodie extended. "What do I have to do?"

"First you've got to quit drinking."

Kenny nodded. "I'll give it my best shot."

"No," Brodie said, "your best shot won't do. You've got to stop."

Rubbing his bleary eyes, Kenny considered his brother's words. "All right."

"Secondly, you've got to move in here where I can keep an eye on you."

"I can't move in here," Kenny protested. "Patsy Ann's staying here. She'll leave if I stay."

"Patsy Ann won't have to know you're here. Not until you've had time to get your act together and find a job. You can stay in the log cabin on the back forty."

Papaw's cabin. Deannie had forgotten about the old place. It was the first house her great-grandfather had built at Willow Creek back in 1893. A tiny honeymoon cabin constructed for him and his new bride.

"Deannie will see to it you get your meals." Brodie jerked his thumb in her direction. "I just hired her as our new housekeeper."

Kenny swung his gaze in her direction, surprise evident

on his face as if noticing her standing in the shadows for the first time.

"Hey," he said, pointing a finger. "You're the one who wiped me out for seven hundred dollars."

Chapter Six

"Help me get him inside." Brodie flashed Deannie a cold stare and hoisted one of Kenny's arms around his shoulder.

Had he heard what his brother had just said? She'd been caught in a lie. She'd told Brodie she was completely broke and now he had discovered she'd won seven hundred dollars from Kenny. Would Brodie fire her? Hitching in her breath, Deannie took a step forward.

"You're a nice-looking woman," Kenny slurred and grinned moonfaced at Deannie when she came around to bolster him on the left side.

"And you're a married man."

"That's true." Kenny bobbed his head. "But maybe not for long."

"Come on, Romeo," Brodie chided, "you can sleep in the house tonight, but tomorrow it's off to the cabin for you."

Deannie cast a glance at Brodie trying hard to read his mind. Was he simply going to let Kenny's comment pass? Could she be so lucky?

"I'll hold him up while you get the door," Brodie said to her, his chilly tone answering her question.

Scurrying to do his bidding, Deannie suddenly felt her dream quickly sliding away. She'd come this far, and now it seemed her long-held goal of seeing her family avenged against the Truebloods was in jeopardy. She had to do something to convince Brodie she wasn't a lying barroom bimbo.

The screen door snapped shut behind them as they maneuvered Kenny through the foyer and into the living room. He leaned heavily against Brodie, causing Brodie to stagger under his brother's weight.

"For crying out loud, Kenny, pick up your feet and try not to breathe on us." Concern mixed with disgust on Brodie's face.

Empathy for the two brothers swirled inside Deannie, confusing her. She easily identified with Brodie's point of view. How many countless times had she helped her inebriated father to bed when he stumbled in at dawn? But in a weird way, she understood Kenny, too. Like her father, he futilely sought refuge to his problems in the bottom of a bottle. Startled, Deannie realized she wanted to help them both.

Since when did she care about a Trueblood? All these years she'd pictured them as worthless scoundrels who'd stolen her home. Now that she'd met them, she realized Brodie and Kenny were just people. Not evil entities hell-bent on destroying her world.

No, the strong voice in her mind reminded her. The same voice that had driven her to practice shuffling cards until her fingers went numb. But Rafe Trueblood ruined your father. Stop being tenderhearted. Weakness will get you nowhere. They don't deserve Willow Creek. The ranch belongs to you and if you have to marry Brodie to get it, then that's what you're going to do.

"Can you make it upstairs?" Brodie asked his brother.

"I think so."

Step by step, they dragged Kenny up the stairs, Deannie struggling to keep up her end of the load and Brodie grimacing often. At last they reached the top, and Brodie directed Kenny to a bedroom on the right.

They dumped Kenny on the bed and he was snoring before he even hit the pillow. Shaking his head, Brodie tugged his brother's boots off and tossed them onto the floor.

Hands clasped behind her back, Deannie started easing toward the door. She wanted to get away from Brodie Trueblood as quickly as possible before he started quizzing her about what Kenny had said out there on the porch.

"I want to speak with you."

Brodie's stern voice halted her escape.

"Me?"

"In the kitchen."

"Now?"

"Yes."

"Can't this wait until morning?" She faked a yawn. "I'm awfully tired."

"No, it can't. I'm going to get Kenny out of his jeans, then I'll be right down."

"Okay." Deannie gulped, a thousand fearful thoughts racing through her mind. At least he hadn't told her to pack her bags. Not yet, anyway.

She waited in the darkened kitchen, her arms crossed over her chest. Moonlight spilled in through the open window, and the breeze stirred the curtains. The clock on the wall chimed eleven. Her moment of truth had arrived.

Ask not for whom the bell tolls.

The floorboards creaked, riveting Deannie's attention to the doorway. Brodie stepped into the room, his face cloaked in shadows. He flicked on the light switch and Deannie blinked against the glare that shone brighter than an interrogator's lamp.

"Who are you?" Brodie demanded.

"Wh-what do you mean? I'm Deannie McCellan," she said, her heart pounding with fear. Did he suspect she was actually Deanna Hollis come to extract her reprisal? Was her stratagem over before it ever started? Deannie gulped, terrified that she was about to be unceremoniously escorted off the grounds of Willow Creek.

"You're a professional gambler, aren't you?" Brodie's tone was harsh, the expression on his face unforgiving. He pushed his fingers through his hair and sighed. "That's why you were in the Lonesome Dove last night. You were hustling poker."

Deannie opened her mouth. This might be the time to come clean. To at least admit to some of the truth. "I'm not a professional gambler," she said.

"If you can take my brother and his cohorts for that amount of money, then you've got to be damned good."

"I'm not too bad."

"You lied to me. You told me you were so broke you couldn't afford to have your car repaired."

"I didn't lie. I am broke."

"What did you do with Kenny's money?"

"I gave it to charity."

Brodie glared at her. "I don't believe you."

"It's the truth."

"Give me one good reason to buy that story."

Deannie stared at her feet. She couldn't tell him why she'd given her ill-gotten winnings to Ester Sweeny at the homeless shelter. Brodie's anger and loss of respect for her, no matter how well deserved, hurt far more than she could imagine.

"There's not a job waiting for you in Santa Fe, is there?" he demanded. "You made that up, too."

Miserably, she shook her head.

"You seem pretty adept at lying and handling drunks. I can tell you've spent your fair share of time in bars." He grasped the back of a chair with both hands. "I've got to tell you, Deannie, that concerns me. I don't know if you're the proper influence for Buster and Angel."

How much could she tell Brodie without giving herself away? She had to say something, or he was going to show her the door.

"I learned to play poker from watching my father," she said. "He had a gambling problem. Drinking problem, too, for that matter."

Brodie nodded grimly. "So you've followed in his footsteps."

"No!" Her vehement denial echoed in the quiet room.

Arching an eyebrow, he waited for her to continue.

"I drink hardly at all and I don't have a gambling problem. Sometimes when I run low on cash I get into a poker game, but that's it. I know what you're thinking, Brodie Trueblood, and you're wrong. I'm not a bar dolly."

"You know," Brodie said, "I'd probably fire you if it weren't for one thing."

She raised a trembling hand to her mouth. "What's that?" she whispered.

"My own father was a professional gambler. I saw first-hand what he did to himself and the people that loved him. He denied he had a problem. He refused to reform. That's why I'm willing to help Kenny. He really wants a better life. And that's why I want to help you, too."

"Brodie…"

"I will insist on one condition, however."

"What's that?"

"I won't tolerate any more lies. From now on you must be completely honest with me."

Feeling like a errant child being scolded for running out into the street, Deannie opened her mouth to speak but didn't. How could she make him a promise she couldn't keep?

"You're a good person, Deannie McCellan, and I intend to rescue you from yourself."

Brodie didn't know whether to believe his head or his heart. His head urged him to forget her, to run as fast as he could in the opposite direction, but his heart cried out for him to accept Deannie at face value. Brodie feared his heart was already falling in love with her.

And that spelled deep trouble.

He also couldn't believe that impromptu speech he had given her. Who was he, the son of a self-proclaimed rascal, to lecture Deannie McCellan about her life?

He sat at the kitchen table, his hands clasped together in front of him. From the moment his family had moved in at Willow Creek, the kitchen had been Brodie's favorite room. His mother had loved to cook, and that's how he remembered her best, standing at the oven creating delicious dishes.

Taking a deep breath, Brodie closed his eyes. He could almost smell her fresh-baked apple pies cooling on the windowsill. If he lingered long enough in the memory, his tongue would begin to tingle with the taste of cinnamon, sugar and flaky crust.

Melinda Trueblood had tried her darnedest to make this house a real home. She'd sewn curtains for the windows and stenciled the walls. She'd cut fresh flowers from her garden and placed them in vases around the house. She had set the table with cheap china dishes, the best she could afford, and had scheduled supper for six-thirty in hopes of generating a normal family routine.

But Rafe had never cooperated, and Kenny was soon following after him, disappearing for days at a time, returning with smug grins and no explanations for their behavior. Mostly it had been Brodie and his mother eating alone at this big table built for twelve.

Sorrow pushed at the back of his eyelids. Brodie swallowed hard and choked off the emotions. There was nothing he could do about the past. He couldn't resurrect his mother, nor could he save his father. The most he could do was make sure such a tragedy never happened to him.

And the only way to ensure that was to avoid women who'd been brought up in dance halls and honky-tonks.

Women like Deannie McCellan.

Brodie opened his eyes and cradled his head in his hands. He was dog tired and bone weary, but sleep evaded him. Why was he so attracted to the one person who could cause him the most grief? Cupid was most definitely a cruel trickster.

He wanted desperately to believe that Deannie was a sweet innocent caught up in the seedy existence her father had fashioned for her. A victim of her parent just as surely as he had been. But part of him, the dark suspicious side, feared that Deannie McCellan was a cold, calculating woman, only out for herself.

He'd witnessed both aspects of her personality.

That night in the Lonesome Dove, perched on a chair next to Kenny under the harsh glare of that bare bulb, she had appeared the epitome of Lady Luck. A beautiful siren luring men to their demise.

But here at the ranch, her devastating red hair caught up in a coltish ponytail, her lustrous peaches-and-cream complexion devoid of makeup, she'd seemed his dream girl. Taking loving care of the children, cooking supper, kissing him with an unprecedented passion. Which persona was the real Deannie McCellan and which was a polished act?

"Damn," Brodie swore under his breath. He'd already promised her she could stay on as their housekeeper. Brodie Trueblood was a man of his word, and unlike his father and brother he honored his obligations. That being the case, one thing was absolutely clear. During the duration of her stay at Willow Creek Ranch, there could be no more physical contact between him and Deannie McCellan. None whatsoever.

Brodie Trueblood actually felt sorry for her? Deannie gave an unladylike snort and flopped over onto her side. She punched her pillow for good measure. As if that man was in any position to pass judgment on her life. He didn't even know who she really was!

He had some gall, assigning himself as her personal savior. She didn't need saving. She just needed her home back.

Calm down, Deannie, getting mad won't solve anything.

That rational thought floated through her brain. True, she should be grateful Brodie hadn't thrown her out the door, effectively ending any schemes she'd been hatching. But as long as they shared the same roof, the chance existed that he would fall in love with her and propose marriage. Too bad Kenny with his big mouth had shown up when he did. Because of that, she would have to wait longer and work even harder to gain Brodie's trust and confidence.

With the current turn of events, Deannie sorely regretted playing poker with Kenny. It had set her back in her endeavor to win Brodie's heart. Had she known Rafe Trueblood would be dead when she came of age, Deannie would never have wasted her time learning how to play poker. If she'd known Brodie Trueblood would be so damned good-looking, that he loathed gambling and that he would be the one to inherit Willow Creek instead of Kenny, she would have instituted her cunning marriage ploy from the very beginning.

But the past was past. She had no choice but to deal with the situation as it existed and hope for the best.

The worst thing she could do at this point was crowd Brodie. He had to believe that by allowing her to work as his housekeeper he was saving her from a life of degradation. She had one option—assume her housekeeping duties with a vengeance, stay on her best behavior and avoid being alone with Brodie Trueblood.

Just because she was forced to maintain a professional relationship with the man, it didn't mean she couldn't use every other seductive tool in her arsenal.

Deannie smiled in the darkness.

She would learn how to cook the best meals he'd ever tasted. She would care for Buster and Angel as if they were her own kids. When Patsy Ann came home from the hospital, she would befriend the woman and become indispensable to her as well. She would clean, she would sew and do her darnedest to prove to Brodie that she could be the perfect wife despite her unorthodox upbringing.

Then, it would only be a matter of time before Brodie Trueblood began longing for the other things a wife could offer. By that time she would have him hook, line and sinker and she would take her rightful place as mistress of Willow Creek.

Good thing Brodie had gotten a big dose of her kisses before Kenny had shown up. Now he knew what he was missing.

Deannie shivered at the memory of those kisses and hugged herself. Problem was, she would be remembering the taste of his mouth as intensely as he would be recalling the flavor of hers.

Come on, Deannie, you've got to stay in control of your emotions. How can you hope to manipulate Brodie into marriage if you allow your hormones to dominate your head?

Manipulate. Such an ugly word. But that was exactly what she was doing.

As if Rafe Trueblood hadn't manipulated your father.

Daddy had been weak and vulnerable after Mama's death, and Rafe had preyed upon his impaired state. Too bad Brodie would have to pay for his father's sins, but someone had to be responsible for the agony that that poor little girl had suffered.

Deannie fisted her hands as the old memories swept through her. Memories that stoked her hunger for revenge. Memories powerful enough to throttle her guilt and urge her onward with her plans.

She remembered that long-ago night as vividly as if fifteen minutes had passed instead of fifteen years.

Bile rose in Deannie's throat, hot and acidic. She had been sleeping in the room down the hall from this one. The room where Buster and Angel now slept.

Back then that room had been decorated entirely in shades of pink, from dusty rose to cotton candy to bubble gum. She'd possessed a canopy bed with a dainty pink coverlet and lace curtains to match. She recalled the rocking chair Daddy had carved by hand, a massive doll collection including twenty-two Barbies, a pink stereo system complete with dozens of cassette tapes and her own Princess phone.

Any little girl's dream.

A dream that had shattered into a nightmare when her daddy had come stumbling into her bedroom, tears streaming down his face.

"Deannie, honey, wake up," he'd said.

Since Mama's death six months earlier, life had become unstable and insecure. Daddy, who used to rise early in the morning and start working the ranch by dawn, now lay in bed until noon. Often he would forget to eat or take a shower. He stopped taking Deannie to church and refused to see friends when they tried to visit.

He'd once been a cheerful man who whistled and sang. Now he frowned frequently and rarely spoke. He began selling off the cattle to pay his debts and he let most of the ranch help go.

Deannie saw her father less and less. He left her in the care of the housekeeper, occasionally for days at a time.

Back then she hadn't really understood what was going on. It was only later she came to realize he'd been gambling and drinking those nights when he disappeared into Yarborough.

"Deannie." Her father had shaken her and turned on the bedside lamp. The muted light had sent shadows jumping across the room. "Come on now, wake up."

Clutching her teddy bear to her chest, her heart pounding, Deannie had scooted up in the bed. Rubbing the sleep from her eyes, she'd stared at the man who'd become a virtual stranger to her. Fear, very similar to what she'd felt when her mother had been killed, clamped a cold hand over her trembling body. Something awful had happened. She knew it.

"Daddy! What's wrong?"

He looked terrible. His eyes were bleary and bloodshot, his clothes rumpled. His hair was in disarray, and he smelled funny. Deannie remembered crinkling her nose in distaste, torn between the desire to hug her father and the repulsion his condition created.

"Get up. Get dressed."

"Why, Daddy? Did someone die?"

"No." Her father threw back the covers. "Get up, Deannie, right this minute."

"Are we going somewhere?" That thought had cheered her temporarily. It would be nice to go on a trip, just her and her daddy.

"Yeah." He'd nodded grimly. "We're going somewhere."

"Where?" Her fear had momentarily slipped away. "To the beach?"

"No." He got on his hands and knees and lifted the dust ruffle on her bed as he searched beneath it. Deannie remembered peering down at him from the bed and noticing the bald spot on the top of his head she'd never remembered seeing before. He pulled out her pink suitcase. It was covered with dust. "Pack your favorite clothes and toys."

His harsh tone brought the fear rippling back.

"Daddy," she'd whispered, curling a hand to her mouth. "You're scaring me."

That's when she'd heard a noise at her bedroom door. Boots scraping the hardwood floor, spurs jangling.

The memory slowed and narrowed in focus. Deannie's throat constricted at the old vision so prominent in her mind. A scene that was as sharp and clear at this moment as it had been the night it played out.

Deannie wadded her pillow in her fists, closed her eyes and tried unsuccessfully to block the memory.

She'd swiveled her head to the doorway. She recalled the stark terror that had driven through her small body at what she'd seen standing there.

A man. Tall, thin, dressed completely in black. He sported a narrow mustache, numerous diamond rings and a wide, gold belt buckle.

Even now, Deannie's blood ran cold and the hair on her forearms raised.

He looked exactly like a silent-movie villain with his dark hair slicked back off his forehead, his thin lips curled smugly at the corners, and his hips cocked in an insouciant pose.

For the first and last time, Deanna Rene Hollis clapped eyes on the man who would forever change her life. The man who'd snatched away her innocence, leaving her bitter and vengeful. The man who'd instilled a hatred inside her so savage it would last fifteen years and spill out onto his sons.

Rafe Trueblood.

He had cocked his head to one side and winked at her. Then he'd pulled a cigar from his front shirt pocket. Striking a match with his thumbnail, he'd lit his cigar and watched her father as he scurried around the room, opening drawers and pulling stuff from the closet.

"Don't get hysterical, Hollis. I told you there was no need for you and your girl to leave tonight. Tomorrow will suit me just fine."

"Daddy?" Her voice had risen high and shrill, more of a demand than a question.

"Hush, Deannie, and get dressed."

"No reason to pull the girl from her bed at midnight."

"Yes there is. Willow Creek doesn't belong to us anymore."

"You're losing it, Hollis. I don't want it being said around Yarborough that I kicked a child out in the middle of the night."

"Perhaps you should have thought about that before you cheated me out of my homestead." Daddy was breathing hard.

Rafe walked across the floor, blowing smoke rings. He thrust his face into Daddy's. "I don't cheat. You stink at poker. It's not my fault you can't hold your liquor and you let your mouth overload your backside."

Deannie coughed and curled her knees up under her chin. She was frozen, welded to her bed, staring at the two men arguing in front of her.

"Did you hear me, Deannie?" her father snarled, spinning away from Rafe and turning to glare at her. "Out of the bed, now!"

"Please, Daddy," she begged, hot tears running down her cheeks. "Tell me why."

Rafe held up a palm. "Please allow me to field this question for you, Hollis."

Her daddy clenched his hands so tight his knuckles turned white.

Smiling, Trueblood stepped toward the bed. "Your daddy bet this ranch and all the contents on a hand of poker. Do you know what that means?"

Deannie shook her head. Rafe Trueblood's breath was warm and smelled worse than her daddy's.

"It means he lost the card game and now Willow Creek belongs to me."

Deannie's bottom lips trembled. "I don't live here anymore? What about my toys and my stereo?"

"I'm sorry, darling, but you're gonna have to leave everything behind. And it's all your daddy's fault."

"You're a cold-blooded snake, Trueblood," her father said, shoving the gambler aside. "Get away from my daughter."

Rafe had chuckled and sauntered out the door, leaving his repulsive scent behind him. "Thanks for the ranch, Hollis," Rafe Trueblood called over his shoulder. "My family was needin' somewhere to live, and this place will do us nicely."

"Daddy?" Deannie had whimpered, stunned and confused by the events she'd just witnessed.

Her father had gone down on his knees in front of her, an agonized expression on his face. He had wrapped his one arm around her and pulled her tight against his chest while his tears dampened her nightgown.

"I'm sorry, baby, so sorry."

"Who is that man, Daddy? Why do we have to leave? Can I take my pony?"

"No, honey, you can't."

"Why?"

"Because, sweetheart, your daddy has gone and done a very stupid thing."

Down the hallway a door clicked closed jerking Deannie from her ghastly reverie. The sound echoed in her ears and issued from the end of the hallway.

Brodie.

Deannie sat up and pushed her hair off her sweat-drenched forehead. The covers lay twisted around her legs, and her heart thundered harder than a West Texas hailstorm. Her mouth was dry and tasted chalky. Her hands trembled and her soul ached.

She glanced at her bedside travel clock. One-thirty and Brodie was still awake. Obviously he had his own demons to contend with.

For the first time in her life, Deannie felt a twinge of sympathy for Brodie Trueblood. As fallible as her own father had been, at least at heart he had been a good person, whereas Rafe Trueblood had been a total blackguard through and through.

Imagine growing up with Rafe for a father. Childhood must not have been easy for Brodie.

But she couldn't allow sympathy for the man to deter her from her real objective. After all, he and his family had taken over her house. They had commandeered her furniture, confiscated her pony, seized the only home she'd ever known and cast her onto the streets.

The old hatred seethed inside her. A hatred that had cut deep and consumed her since she was seven years old. A hatred that had shaped her into the woman she was today. Strong, scornful, full of rage.

She still wanted revenge.

No, it was more than that. She demanded revenge. Needed it, ached after it, thirsted after the sweet satisfaction of knowing she'd avenged her father. If she regained Willow Creek, then Gil Hollis wouldn't have died for nothing.

The blame lay in one place and one place only. At the feet of Rafe Trueblood. And now that he was gone, his sons would have to serve as proxy, bearing the responsibility for the sins of their father. It might not be fair, but what was fair about tossing a defenseless child from her home because her father had lost a card game?

Well, she wasn't defenseless anymore. The Truebloods had better get ready. Retribution was near, and the time had come to pay the piper.

Swinging her legs over the edge of the bed, Deannie sat

there a moment, trying to get her wrath under control before she trekked across the hallway to the bathroom. She panted against the thick, heavy sensation in her chest.

Coming back to Willow Creek had unearthed dormant memories and rock-hard emotions. She'd known that returning would dredge up those ugly feelings, but Deannie had to admit the actual reality was far more shocking than she'd anticipated.

She stared at the square of moonlight seeping through the window and onto the carpet and fought hard to suppress the tears welling in her throat. Crying would get her nowhere. Pleading would do no good. Weeping, she'd discovered on that awful night so long ago, was for cowards and sissies like her father.

Deannie clenched her jaw. Not she. She was not her father's daughter. She was a fighter, a survivor. She refused to give in to defeat no matter how the odds seemed stacked against her.

She would not fail. Somehow, someway, through hook or by crook, she would wrest Willow Creek Ranch back from the Truebloods if it took her dying breath to achieve that goal!

Chapter Seven

Deannie steered Brodie's four-wheel-drive pickup truck across the back pasture. He had given her the keys that morning along with a hand-drawn map to help her locate the log cabin. She didn't need instructions. She remembered exactly where Papaw's old cabin sat nestled among the willow trees flanking the creek bank.

Brodie promised to meet her at the cabin by nine o'clock to help her get things organized. With Patsy Ann scheduled to come home from the hospital tomorrow, they didn't have much time to get the place cleaned and readied for occupancy. Kenny had taken Angel and Buster into town with him, freeing Deannie to accomplish the chore.

At breakfast, Brodie had acted very cool and indifferent toward her. Deannie accepted his mood, knowing she had to give him breathing room. Last night's events had strengthened her resolve. She would wait forever if that's what it took to make Brodie Trueblood fall in love with her and propose marriage.

A chaparral darted from the tall johnsongrass and raced along beside the truck as she guided the vehicle over rough brushy terrain. Cattle grazed on both sides of the makeshift road. White-faced Herefords on the left, black Angus on the right. A windmill, old but still functional, spun listlessly beside the stock tank. Along the fence row, giant sunflowers grew in wild abandon.

Deannie rolled down the window and took in a deep breath of home. Scissortails flitted on the telephone lines, and killdeers cried from the mesquite trees. Nostalgia mixed with regret. The emotions rose inside her, knotting hard and pressing relentlessly against her rib cage until she had difficulty catching her breath.

She'd lost so much. Not just her home but her heritage as well. When she should have been spending her childhood shinnying up trees and catching tadpoles in the pond, she'd been wandering through back alleys looking for aluminum cans to sell, and sleeping on pool tables in smoky bars waiting for her daddy to cash in his chips and go home.

"Damn you, Rafe Trueblood, for stealing my life," Deannie muttered, fisting one hand in her lap. "But you'll pay," she vowed. "I'll have the last laugh."

And hurt Brodie in the process.

Those words floated through Deannie's mind, but she trampled them down along with her guilt. Brodie Trueblood was a big boy and he could take care of himself. She wouldn't allow misguided sympathy to stand in the way of what she wanted. Had Brodie felt sorry for her when he and his family had usurped her home?

She drove over a rise and spotted Papaw's log cabin in the distance, partially hidden by willow trees.

The nostalgia intensified and Deannie brushed a tear from her cheek. None of that, she chided herself, but her chest squeezed tighter.

She bumped across the trickling creek and rode over a clump of smooth, flat rocks. Brodie's truck easily scaled the craggy territory. It was a brand-new pickup, this year's model, complete with all the whistles and bells. Electric windows and doors, an expensive stereo and compact disc player, extended cab, reclining leather bucket seats. Hardly a work vehicle. Obviously the man wasn't suffering for money if he utilized such a fine automobile for day-to-day ranching.

I'll get half of his fortune, too, when I divorce him.

Deannie frowned. That idea brought no pleasure. She wasn't after Brodie's money. He'd made that on his own, and she had no claim to it. She would let him keep every red cent. He could have the cattle and sheep, as well. All she wanted was her Willow Creek.

Pulling up to the cabin, she sat there a moment, gathering her courage to face what lay ahead. Her gaze scanned the yard. Weeds had taken over the spot where Great-grandma used to work a vegetable garden. Deannie could almost taste the vine-ripened tomatoes, crisp ears of baby corn and savory black-eyed peas. Her mouth watered. Store-bought produce had never rivaled home-grown.

The front screen door hung on one hinge and aged farming equipment rusted beside a decrepit chicken coop long since devoid of poultry. An old-fashioned hand pump was positioned over a water trough around the side of the house, a white salt lick squatting beside it. A few boards in the corral had recently been replaced, the bright brown wood a stark contrast against the gray, weathered fencing.

Killing the engine, Deannie took a deep breath and got out of the truck. A jackrabbit leaped up from behind a cactus, tall ears twitching, his powerful hind legs propelling him across the prairie at lightning quick speed. Startled, Deannie stumbled backward, muttering under her breath. She should have worn boots instead of her sneakers. What if that rabbit had been a rattlesnake?

She glanced at her watch. Ten minutes until nine. Brodie would be here soon.

After retrieving cleaning supplies from the truck bed, Deannie headed up the stone path leading to the cabin.

Juggling the mop, broom, bucket, soap and bleach, she nudged the screen door open with her toe. The reluctant metal shrieked in protest.

A musty odor greeted her when she entered the cabin. A fine layer of dust covered everything—cardboard boxes, sheet-draped furniture, brown paper sacks, steamer trunks. The tiny house was jam-packed with junk. Evidently, Brodie used the cabin as storage space.

Whew. Deannie rested her hands on her hips and surveyed the gathered chaos. They certainly had their work cut out for them.

"Quite a mess, isn't it?"

The sound of Brodie Trueblood's voice sent chills rippling through her. Chills of desire, apprehension or downright fear, Deannie couldn't say which. She set down her burden and turned on her heels to face him.

Clearly he hadn't gotten much sleep. Dark circles ringed his eyes, and his cheeks appeared drawn and gaunt. He held his shoulders stiff, as if afraid to relax in her presence.

Even weary he was still the most handsome man she'd ever seen. Not necessarily in the slick, polished fashion Hollywood defined as handsome. No. Brodie's attractiveness was much more than skin-deep. It was in the way he walked, the way he held himself. His voice, strong and deep, heightened his masculinity. And his slightly irregular features were far more intriguing than any flawless face.

"I didn't hear you drive up," Deannie said, nervously running a hand through her hair.

"I rode Ranger."

"Oh."

A curtain of silence settled over them. Deannie flicked her gaze around the room, desperately searching for something to focus on. Anything to keep from looking into Brodie Trueblood's disturbing brown eyes. Knowing eyes that seemed to peer straight into her soul.

Butterflies flitted in her stomach. She had to hold her

goal firmly in mind—make Brodie fall in love with her. Deannie knew she possessed the physical attributes required, but she had to proceed carefully. Brodie's guard would be up. She had to find small ways to seduce him. Anything overt was bound to send him running in the opposite direction.

Think, Deannie, what does Brodie care about? Willow Creek Ranch, Angel and Buster, Patsy Ann, his brother. Home and family. There lay the battlefield. If she was to win his heart, she had to appeal to his love for the land and his hunger for roots.

"We better get to work." Brodie nodded curtly, effectively derailing her thoughts.

"Where do we start?" Deannie asked, overwhelmed by the task facing them.

"I'll stuff these boxes and crates into the bedrooms. That'll make room in here."

"What'll we do about the bedrooms?"

"Kenny can sleep on the fold-out couch."

"I think it's admirable," Deannie said softly, "what you're doing for your brother." She might be deceiving him, but she wasn't lying to him. She did believe Brodie to be an honorable man.

So why are you so set on cheating him?

Because there was no other way to get back Willow Creek. Damn, it was hard having a conscience. Too bad she wasn't as cold-blooded as Rafe Trueblood. Actually it was too bad Rafe wasn't alive so she could obtain her retaliation face-to-face and leave Brodie out of it all together.

Deannie had to stop viewing her plan as cheating Brodie. She must keep her perspectives firmly in mind and not be swayed by her fascination with him. She had to perceive her calculated machinations as balancing the score, settling a fifteen-year-old debt. That was the only way she could see the deception through to its conclusion.

Brodie didn't reply. Instead, he grasped a box and headed

for the back room. Not knowing what else to do, Deannie gathered up two paper sacks and followed suit, knocking loose a dust shower in the process.

The bedroom was small and almost as packed as the living room. It housed two twin beds stacked high with clutter. The peculiar assortment included Christmas decorations: multicolored twinkle lights, two plastic lawn Santas, a green and red felt tree skirt; yards and yards of unused material in a variety of faded colors and moth-eaten fabrics, and a wide collection of paperback books from Louis L'Amour Westerns to romance novels.

"Stack it anywhere," Brodie said, waving a hand.

"Where did this stuff come from?" Deannie asked, wrinkling her nose to suppress a sneeze.

"Most of it belonged to the previous owners."

Deannie froze, her fingers still curled around the sack. Some of her old possessions could be here!

"Some of it was my mother's…"

Brodie's eyes fixed on an object in the corner and his voice took on a husky tone and trailed off longingly. Deannie tracked his gaze and spied a carousel music box resting on top of an oak bureau.

He moved across the hardwood floor, his boots making a rough clipping noise. His hand closed around the music box and cradled it gently. In that moment Deannie realized just how much his mother had meant to him.

His large fingers looked incongruous turning that tiny key. He wound it completely then sat the music box back down on the bureau. She noticed he held his breath and that his hands trembled ever so slightly.

The music box sprang to life, the carousel horses twirling around the base as they moved up and down their poles. A tinny melody filled the air, Deannie cocked her head, trying to recognize the tune.

"Skater's Waltz."

The haunting chords echoed sadly throughout the room and tugged at her heart.

Brodie jammed his hands into his pockets and watched the carousel horses prance.

"My mother loved that music box," he said softly. "I bought it for her the Christmas I turned twelve. I mowed lawns all summer and raked leaves in the fall to pay for it."

His quiet revelation provided Deannie further insight into Brodie's psyche. Much-needed information she could use in her campaign to draw closer to him. His mother had been the one to keep him on the straight and narrow. She had given him his strength of character. Their obviously loving relationship had prevented Brodie from taking after Rafe as Kenny had done.

Deannie cleared her throat. "Your mother must have meant a lot to you."

A hooded expression shuttered his eyes. "We were close."

"How did she die?"

"Cancer. She was only forty-two."

"I'm sorry."

Brodie raised his head and looked at her. She saw pain reflected in his eyes. Deep, inconsolable.

"I built Willow Creek into what it is today as a tribute to her," he said. "You can see why this place means so much to me."

If only you knew how much this place means to me, too!

"Yes," Deannie replied. "I can understand. My mother died when I was seven."

"How?"

He'd warned her last night not to lie to him, but what could she do? If she told him her mother had been killed in a riding accident, he just might remember how Gil Hollis's wife died and start to put two and two together. He was already suspicious of her, and Brodie Trueblood was not a stupid man.

"She had cancer, too," she lied.

"So you do know how I feel." Compassion lit his eyes.

Deannie looked away, unable to bear Brodie's sympathy.

It was strange that Willow Creek had played an important role in both their lives. Coming to live here had given Brodie a sense of purpose, driving him to excel, while being torn from this ranch had supplied Deannie with an equally insatiable desire to reclaim it as her own.

Walking the short distance across the crowded room, she laid a hand on his shoulder. "I think your mother would be very proud of what you've done with Willow Creek."

Their gazes sealed. Something unspoken passed between them. A silent cognition that bound them together.

"We don't have time to waste talking," Brodie said suddenly, shaking off her hand. "Let's get back to work."

"Okay," she replied, startled and oddly hurt by the abrupt change in his demeanor.

"I think you should concentrate on cleaning the place. I'll handle the lifting and moving."

"All right," she conceded, knowing better than to push.

Stalking past her, Brodie left the room, leaving Deannie to ponder what she'd done to upset him so.

In spite of his best intentions, he was letting Deannie McCellan get too close. Brodie hefted another box onto his shoulder and carted it into the bedroom.

He couldn't afford to let things progress so swiftly. He didn't know enough about her, and what he did know was not very commendable.

"Cool your jets, Trueblood," he muttered under his breath. "There's plenty of time for things to develop. No hurry. No rush."

So why did a headlong urgency consume him whenever he was around Deannie? Why had thoughts of her kept him awake all night? Why did he fantasize about the taste of those luscious pink lips when he was fully aware of the dangers involved?

Yes, his head said, slow down, slow down, slow down. But his heart cried, now, now, now.

Brodie stacked the box alongside the others, placed his palms against his lower back and stretched.

The truth of the matter was that he was simply very vulnerable at this juncture in his life. His father had just died, and even though they'd never seen eye to eye, a part of his past was dead and buried for good. Some mourning was required.

Also, he was the one who had inherited Willow Creek. Complete responsibility for the ranch's success or failure officially lay at his feet. Brodie had to provide not only for himself but also for Kenny and his family.

There were adjustments to be made and needs to satisfy. Needs that had been gnawing at Brodie for a long time. The sharp, aching need to find a wife, get married and produce heirs of his own. What was the objective in pouring his heart into Willow Creek if he had no one to leave it to.

Brodie bit his bottom lip. How he longed for a chance to be a better father to his children than Rafe had been to him. Raising happy, healthy children would be one method of atoning for his father's sins.

"Block it out. Think about it later," he told himself.

"Did you say something?" Deannie inquired sweetly when he returned to the living room. She glanced up from where she was sweeping dust balls out the front door.

Mid-morning sunlight splashed into the cabin, catching her fiery red hair in a shining glow. She appeared almost angelic standing there with that halo of curls tumbling around her head, and the corners of her mouth tugged upward.

His stomach clenched in response to her smile. "Nothing," he mumbled.

The air smelled of soap and bleach, and Brodie wondered if the odor might account for his attack of dizziness. He hated to think it might be Deannie's proximity.

She continued her sweeping, her lithe body moving in a hypnotic rhythm.

Whish, whish, whish. The broom scooted across the wood.

They were dressed alike, Brodie noted with a start. Both were wearing white cotton T-shirts now streaked with dirt, and faded blue jeans. The only difference was he had on boots and she'd donned sneakers. It was as if their minds ran along the same track. She was a feminine version of himself.

No. She's very different from you. Remember, you found her in a bar. She's more like Kenny or Rafe.

Yet despite his own protests, Brodie couldn't shake the notion that she was his mirror image. His other half.

He watched Deannie, mesmerized by her lithe motion. How beguiling she looked, those faded denims hugging her fanny tighter than a lover's passionate embrace, her face scrubbed free of cosmetics. It took every ounce of control he could muster not to cross that floor, whisk her into his arms and kiss her.

Brodie didn't know how much more of this temptation he could tolerate. How much longer could he keep his distance before he had to ask her to leave to preserve his own sanity? Yet she'd done nothing to lead him on. It wasn't her fault she caused such a reaction in him. He couldn't toss her out on the streets. If he did and she went back to gambling and hanging out in bars and God knew what else, then he would be accountable. Dammit, he should be man enough to master his surging testosterone. Deannie shouldn't be made to suffer for his weaknesses.

"There," she said, rubbing her palms together. "That's a start."

"Huh?" He blinked, thankful she was completely unaware of the direction in which his mind had traveled.

"I'll tackle the kitchen next. I've got an hour before I have to be back at the farmhouse to cook lunch."

Deannie tucked a lock of hair behind one perfect seashell-shaped ear, and that utterly innocent gesture with provocative overtones had Brodie yearning to nibble at her delectable lobes.

"Are you okay?" She squinted at him.

"Yeah. Fine." Nothing wrong except he was about to explode with suppressed passion. "Well, maybe that bleach smell is getting to me," he replied, grasping at any plausible excuse. "Think I'll take a walk outside and get some fresh air."

"It is kinda overpowering," Deannie agreed. "Maybe I'll come with you."

"No," Brodie practically shouted, holding up both palms. The hurt expression on her face cut him to the quick. "I mean, my stomach's a little queasy, and I'd hate for you to see me get sick."

With that pathetic explanation, he rushed out the front door.

Funny, his gut did feel jittery. He suspected, however, that his affliction had nothing to do with the bleach and everything to do with Deannie McCellan.

Why was he so drawn to her? It had to be more than physical attraction. He'd met many beautiful women in his twenty-nine years on the planet and none had ever upset his apple cart like Deannie did. Was it their similar backgrounds? Both had fathers who were gamblers, both lost their mothers at a young age. Could mere empathy create such a dynamic sensation?

Or could it be more? Was there an inexplicable something that poets wrote poems about and artists created paintings over? Could love at first sight be possible, and was there indeed such a thing as one man for one woman?

Even considering it caused foreign churnings somewhere in the region of his heart.

Shaking his head, Brodie strode over to the corral where he'd tied Ranger. The gelding neighed a greeting.

Brodie scratched Ranger behind the ears. The horse's companionship helped ground him in reality. Ranching was his life. Willow Creek was his home. He'd worked so hard to obtain this place he couldn't jeopardize it for the first female to ever command his full attention. But denying Deannie's powerful charisma was far harder than he imagined.

He glanced back over his shoulder at the cabin. She'd disappeared from the door, and Brodie experienced a peculiar sensation of loss. How could it be that she'd come to mean so much to him in such a short period of time?

When he'd told her about his mother, she'd listened quietly, a sad pensive look upon her face. She'd been so receptive, he'd felt as if he could tell her anything. That fact alone was enough to scare the hell out of him. He'd always been closemouthed and secretive with his private thoughts. Without even encouraging him, Deannie had elicited emotions he'd never expressed. Not to anyone.

Dang. He had to cease thinking about her like this. Maybe a ride around the perimeter would empty his head.

He swung into the saddle and wheeled Ranger west. The sun, perched high in the sky, beat down warm and cheerful. Brodie readjusted his hat to shade his eyes.

It wasn't fair of him to leave Deannie inside the cabin doing all the cleaning for his brother's benefit, but Brodie just could not face her at this moment. Not while they were out here all alone. One glance into those ice blue eyes and he would be a goner for sure.

A bonus. He would pay her a bonus to ease his conscience.

Ranger tossed his head as if in agreement. Brodie kneed the gelding in the ribs, urging him into a trot.

The horse surged forward. Grasshoppers sprang up in their wake. Brodie leaned low in the saddle, guiding Ranger west of the cabin and toward the creek.

Brodie had come here often when the family had first moved in at Willow Creek. The cabin, the creek, the willow trees had been his refuge from Rafe. That old familiar feeling of safety washed over him as Ranger traveled the creek bed, spindly willow branches slapping lightly against Brodie's legs.

Ranger's hooves kicked up a fine spray from the thin creek, splashing his face and cooling down the sizzle Deannie McCellan had produced inside him.

"He-ya!" Brodie called, swatting the gelding on the rump.

Ranger sprang into a gallop. By this point, they had almost completely circled the cabin. Unable to stop himself, Brodie cast another glance at the front door.

And saw her.

Oblivious to his presence, Deannie was scrubbing the windows inside the cabin. The tip of her pink tongue was caught between her teeth, and a narrow frown cut a path across her brow as she concentrated on the job at hand.

Brodie stared.

Deannie stretched, reaching high to get the top panes. Her breasts, pert and firm, thrust forward, straining against her thin cotton T-shirt. Her nipples, hard as pebbles, pushed upward with the motion.

The sight generated a swift response inside him. Immediate pressure rose below his belt, erecting an aching ballast against his zipper.

His mouth fell open. He gripped the saddle horn and the reins slipped from his astonished fingers.

Ranger pitched up the creek bed, his hooves striking the

rocks. Before Brodie could regain control, a branch whacked him in the face, knocking him off balance.

Brodie tumbled backward.

His arms flailed. His fingers grasped at air. He came up with a fistful of willow leaves and landed smack dab on his backside.

In a cactus patch.

"Yeow!" Brodie howled.

His hat flew behind him. His boots hit the soft dirt, heels digging in deep. He tried to struggle to his feet, but squirming only served to drive the spines deeper into his rear end. He stopped moving and panted against the pain.

"Brodie!" Deannie shouted. She dashed out the front door and ran toward him.

Strangely enough, just seeing her assuaged the sting. He watched her fly across the ground, with what he knew was a dopey expression on his face. Worry made her eyes shiny and her chest heave as she breathed in short, rapid gasps.

"I saw you fall," she exclaimed when she reached him. "Are you all right?"

"Except for the cactus in my posterior, I'm fine."

"Oh, dear!" Deannie's eyes widened as she realized where he had landed.

Brodie extended her his hand. "Could you help me up, please?"

Nodding, she braced herself and tugged on his arm.

Brodie winced at the sharpness shooting through his backside. He pushed up and she hauled him to a standing position.

She took a tentative step around him and stared down at his bottom. "Oh, my gosh," she whispered. "You're covered in thorns."

"Tell me about it," Brodie muttered.

Peeking back at his face, her mouth widened into a circle of concern. "What are we going to do?"

"There's a first aid kit in the pickup. Hopefully there's some tweezers in it."

Brodie took a stiff step forward. A thousand tiny stickers pricked his skin. He hissed in a deep breath, excruciatingly aware of the embarrassing nature of his situation. Deannie was going to have to pluck the thorns from his butt.

Groaning more from that thought than from the pain, Brodie took another step.

"Goodness." Deannie laid her palms on either side of her cheeks in a gesture of disquiet. "I can't hardly stand to watch you."

"Aw," he said. "I've been through much worse than this."

Quit sniveling, Trueblood and get over to the cabin, Brodie chided. He couldn't have Deannie thinking him a wimp.

Mentally cinching himself against the barbed discomfort, he fixed a stoic mask on his face. Marching toward the house, head held high, his blue jeans chafing against the bristles with every movement, Brodie swore under his breath.

"I'll get the first aid kit," Deannie volunteered, and hurried over to the truck.

The pickup's door slammed behind him and Deannie's feet slapped against the stone sidewalk as she caught up with him.

"Got it," she said.

He nodded, not really in the mood for conversation.

"Where are we gonna do this at?" Deannie asked once they entered the cabin. Brodie blinked in the dim coolness that contrasted with the brightness outside and the throbbing in his rear end.

Closing his eyes briefly, Brodie gulped. Where indeed?

"The couch will do," he replied, surprised to hear his words sounded sort of strangled. Whether it was from the pain or from what was about to happen next, he couldn't say.

Deannie tightened her hand around the first aid kit and made a face. "How are we going to get your pants off?"

"Do I have to take them off?"

"Brodie, how do you expect me to pluck those spines out through denim?"

She had a point. He drew in a sigh.

"I don't want to expose myself to you," he said. "I mean you shouldn't have to see a man's bare backside." *Oh, Lord, that didn't come out right.*

"I know this isn't pleasant, but I'm the only one here to do it. You certainly can't climb back on Ranger or ride in the truck to the farmhouse. Can you imagine bumping across the fields in your condition?"

Brodie gritted his teeth. No, he couldn't. "All right. I'll try to get the jeans off."

"While you're doing that I'll check the first aid kit for tweezers," she said.

"Good idea." Feeling like an A-number-one fool, Brodie turned his back to her.

Deannie focused her gaze on the first aid kit. Her vision narrowed to the large red cross gracing the front of the white plastic box. All moisture disappeared from her mouth.

Her eyes might have been fixed on that kit as if it were a lifeline, but her ears were acutely attuned to every noise Brodie Trueblood was creating from across the room. Crazy, seductive, getting naked noises.

The sound of his belt unbuckling sent shivers skating down her spine. She heard the belt slither as he whipped it from the loops. Next came the snap. It popped loud as a firecracker in her sensitive ears. His zipper, easing down the track inch by painful inch made a whispering noise that whooshed in her ears like the wild ocean tide during a lunar eclipse. Heat swamped her entire body. She was about to see Brodie Trueblood's bare behind in all its radiant glory.

Oh dear, oh dear, oh dear. What had she gotten herself

into? Truth was, she'd never seen a nude man. This would be a first for her.

Deannie's fingers fumbled with the first aid kit's clasp. The ornery thing wouldn't budge. Her hands were thick with sweat and a trickle of perspiration rolled down her cheek, plopping onto her shirt.

Calm down, chill out, cool it. Don't you dare blow this, Deanna Rene Hollis. This is a primo opportunity to ingratiate him to you. Remember the old fable of "Androcles and the Lion?" Androcles removed the thorn from the lion's paw and earned the animal's undying gratitude.

"You find the tweezers?" Brodie asked.

"Uh, I'm just having a little trouble getting this thing open. Are you ready?"

"I have to shimmy my jeans down."

At that visual image, she yanked on the lock and the kit sprang open, sending gauze and scissors and ointment flying across the room. Scrambling along the floor on her hands and knees in pursuit of the escaping supplies, she finally located the tweezers peeking out from under the edge of the couch.

"Got 'em." She waved the metal instruments in the air.

"Let's get this over with," Brodie said in the resigned tone of a man sentenced to die in the gas chamber.

Deannie kept her head tastefully turned while Brodie carefully shucked his jeans. He groaned a couple of times in the process but all in all she thought he handled the pain pretty well.

"Ready."

She turned to find him lying on his stomach across the couch, his underwear still on. Bright red bikini briefs. Deannie had to slap a hand over her mouth to keep from guffawing at the picture he presented. She would never have figured straitlaced Brodie Trueblood as a man who favored bikini briefs. Especially red ones. Obviously he had a deeply sensual side she knew nothing about.

"Are you going to leave your underwear on?"

"Yes!" he snapped.

"Okay." Good. She didn't think she could survive witnessing that firm tush completely unclothed. "I'm gonna need more light."

"There's a lamp in the bedroom."

"Be right back," she said, willing her heart to stop racing.

She hurried to the bedroom, retrieved the lamp, then returned to plug it in next to the sofa. She dropped to her knees beside him, her eyes level with his distracting derriere. Squinting, she gazed along that finely honed muscular plane.

"Whew, there sure are lots of them. I don't know where to start plucking."

"For pity's sake, Deannie, grab one and yank it out," he said, his voice muffled from having his face thrust into the couch cushion. "They hurt like hell."

Her fingers quivered as she grasped the tweezer. Leaning over, she rested her elbow on the back of his knees to stabilize her hand. Squinting, she inspected his excellently proportioned bottom.

The fine white quills stood out against the red cotton material. There were dozens. Over a hundred maybe. This could take forever. Deannie swallowed hard.

Despite her best intentions to concentrate on the job at hand, she couldn't help noticing his finely corded leg muscles and how his thighs curved enticingly into his hips. He smelled rather delicious, too, like leather and sand and horses. Most definitely the odor of home. The aroma she'd craved for the past fifteen years.

"Deannie! What's the problem?"

"I'm scared of hurting you."

"Just do it." He sounded rather irritated.

"Okay. Here goes nothing."

Tweezers posed, she jerked out an offending spine.

Brodie grunted. "Keep going."

Depositing it into the lid of the first aid kit, Deannie then tackled another one.

His skin burned warm beneath her arm. The hair on his legs glowed dark and thick. Deannie tried not to notice such things but it was impossible. He was too much man to deny.

She forgot to breathe.

Her entire body underwent an incredible metamorphosis. Her head swam. Her pulse accelerated. Her nipples hardened. Her tummy melted. Her toes curled and her heart sang.

One thought and one thought only pounded in her brain. *I want to make love with Brodie Trueblood.*

Chapter Eight

Brodie was in agony. Not from the cactus spines, but from Deannie's hot breath torching a hole through his posterior. He couldn't stand much more of this.

It was a darn good thing he was lying on his stomach or she would be very shocked to discover exactly what thoughts were bouncing around his head, causing some very physical reactions.

Her soft skin brushing against the back of his legs, her glorious magnolia scent badgering his nostrils, the quiet little tsk-tsking sounds she made with her tongue served to drive him batty.

Remember, Trueblood, she's a gambler's daughter with a questionable past. You can't let your hormones rule your head.

Then a startling notion hit him. What if Deannie felt the very same way about him? What if she were hesitant to acknowledge *her* feelings because *he* was a gambler's son with an unsavory background?

Closing his eyes, Brodie groaned into the pillow.

Deannie hissed in a breath. "I'm sorry. Did I hurt you?"

"Don't stop." It already seemed as if they'd been here for eons, he wanted this over and done with.

"I got all the big ones, but there's still lots of little ones I can barely see through your underwear."

She ran a finger over the spot where the thorns were thickest. A million pinpricks shot through his nerve endings.

"Ouch!" He arched his back against the pain. "What in the heck are you doing?"

"I'm feeling them since I can't see them." She sounded more than a little irked with him. He considered that the task was only slightly less odious on her end.

"Well, cut it out, that hurts like the dickens."

"Brodie," Deannie said huskily, "there's simply no way around it. I'm going to have to push your underwear out of the way in order to get the rest of them."

He gritted his teeth. "Do what you have to do."

Her nimble fingers curled around the elastic at his leg. Her fingernails lightly scratched the area where his thigh merged with his buttocks. Awareness fused with discomfort, and Brodie wondered whether he had died and this was his punishment in hell—a beautiful, sexy woman raising his undies so she could pick stickers from his bare rump.

"There," she said, "that's much better."

He could tell she was keeping the cotton material pushed upward with one hand while she continued to extract thorns with the other. He'd never been in a more embarrassing situation.

The overhead ceiling fan blew cool air against his bare skin, but Brodie burned so hot inside, he scarcely noticed.

Time stretched, elongating into slow motion. He experienced each of Deannie's measured movements in excruciating minutiae. The tip of the metal tweezers poked and prodded. Her breath whistled softly as she inhaled through clenched teeth. Her aroma, like large white flowers blooming in the spring sunshine, dominated his senses.

"I think I got them all," she crowed, triumphant at long last.

Hallelujah!

"Here, let me check." Tentatively Brodie reached a hand around behind him and gingerly fingered his rear end. The area was raw, tender but he felt no more biting stings.

He knew Deannie had rocked back on her heels and was observing him, while still holding his underwear aloft for his explorations.

His finger struck something. "Oooh, there's one."

"Hang on, I'll get it."

A twinge, then it was gone.

"Check again," she said.

He repeated his maneuvers, this time gratefully coming up free and clear of any more cactus splinters.

"Now for the antibiotic ointment," she said.

"I'll do it," Brodie said, hastily taking the ointment from her. He applied it quickly and then pushed himself to a sitting position, desperate to hide his bottom from her sight.

Deannie moved to sit beside him. "Still sore."

"Yeah, but you got all the thorns." Knowing his face was as crimson as his underwear, Brodie avoided meeting her eyes. "Thanks. I know it wasn't pleasant for you, either."

"Oh, I don't know about that," she drawled, the sound of her voice sending a shudder through his groin. "I've certainly had worse chores and without the splendid view."

Holy smokes! He was in deep and getting deeper.

"Don't be so mortified, Brodie. It could happen to anyone."

"Well," he replied, "this wasn't the way I imagined you'd get to see my backside."

"Oh?"

He sneaked a fast peek at her and saw a teasing smile

curl her lips. One cocky eyebrow perched on her forehead, and her blue eyes danced with mirth.

"No." He chuckled, helpless to resist her flirtation.

"How *did* you imagine it?"

"Um...er...you know," he stammered. Was it possible for any one man's face to blister a darker red? Brodie ducked his head. "I better get dressed." He cleared his throat, unable to continue in the kidding vein he'd inadvertently established.

He reached across the floor for his jeans.

"Wait a minute, there might be some thistles remaining in your pants," she cautioned. "Let me check them out for you."

He handed her his pants and settled back down on the couch. He wanted to pace the floor, to thread his fingers through his hair, to dash from the room, anything to deal with the emotions running riot in his brain.

But he couldn't. He had no pants.

Deannie held his jeans under the lamp, squinting and running her fingers lightly across the seat, intently searching for cactus thorns. Watching, Brodie gulped.

That's how she'd appeared, hovering over his behind, he realized. Her mouth twisted into a studious expression, her curly red hair trailing down her shoulders, her slender fingers moving gracefully as she worked.

In that moment she reminded him of Mama. Brodie remembered his mother sitting in her favorite chair at night, doing the mending. They didn't have money for new clothes, their outfits were hand-me-downs from neighbors or stuff Mama picked up at Goodwill or the Salvation Army for a dollar. Consequently, most of the garments required repair—hems taken up, buttons sewn on, rips patched.

An overwhelming tenderness swept over Brodie as he watched Deannie. An intense emotion unlike anything he'd ever experienced. Before he could stop himself, before he could think twice, Brodie leaned over and kissed her.

Lightly, gently, sweetly on the cheek.

Deannie looked up. Surprise widened her eyes.

Whisked away on the headiness of the moment, Brodie put his arm around her and drew her closer. Sitting here in his underwear, he felt vulnerable yet strangely free as if his inhibitions had disappeared along with the cactus quills.

Deannie smelled so fine, felt so good in his embrace, he had to taste her. Dipping his head, he angled for her lips.

She didn't hesitate, nor did she encourage him. She simply waited for him to make the next move.

That mouth, soft and inviting, lured him forward. Her teeth parted sightly.

With a hungry growl, he took up occupancy in her mouth. Closing his eyes against the onslaught of erotic sensations zipping through his system, Brodie clung to her, drinking the delicious nectar that was Deannie McCellan. No woman had ever made him feel so vibrant, so manly, so alive.

He kissed her again and again. Her moistness suffused him with a heretofore undreamed of sustenance. It was as if he'd spent his whole life eating peanut butter and stale crackers when he could have been dining on lobster, steak and caviar.

Suddenly Deannie pressed both palms against his chest and pushed. "What did you do that for?" she whispered.

Brodie drew back as confused by his behavior as she. It was as if he'd been trapped in a magic spell, unable to understand what was happening or alter his actions.

"I don't know. I just wanted to kiss you."

Tears misted her eyes and she lowered her head. Was she going to cry? Why? He hadn't meant to offend her.

"Deannie?" He reached out, cupped her chin in his hand and forced her to look him in the eyes. "Are you upset with me?"

She shook her head. Vehemently.

"What's wrong."

"Nothing."

"Talk to me. Please."

"You're so nice," she said, her voice almost a sob.

"That's a problem?"

She waved a hand, liquid pooling at the corners of her eyes.

"You're used to abusive guys? Is that it?" The thought that someone had mistreated her jammed his gut with anger.

"No."

"Come on," he coaxed, wiping away one tear that slid down her cheek. "Tell me."

"I thought you said we weren't supposed to touch."

He nodded. "I did. But then you were forced to pluck spines out of my backside, and I'd say that was definitely an intimate act that changed all the rules."

"Don't lead me on, Brodie Trueblood," she said.

He stared at her. She had a point. He'd been waffling, sending mixed messages. Last night he'd issued a strictly hands-off policy, today he'd sneaked a kiss.

"You're right," he said. "I was out of line."

Disappointment shone on her face. What had she expected of him? Logically, mentally, he wasn't ready to take their relationship to a higher plane. They didn't know enough about each other even if Deannie McCellan had seen every mole and bump on his backside. But emotionally, physically, he longed to have her welded to his side.

A car horn tooted outside the cabin, causing them both to jump. Brodie vaulted off the couch and hurried to the window.

"Good gosh," he exclaimed. "It's Kenny and the kids. Give me my jeans. Now. Quick. This instant!"

The next day, Buster, Angel, Deannie and Brodie brought Patsy Ann and the new baby home from the hospital. Ensconced in the cabin, and nervous about seeing his wife, Kenny stayed behind.

Deannie and Brodie hadn't spoken since his brother and the children had interrupted their tête-à-tête the morning before. In fact, avoiding each other had become their favorite activity. Brodie hadn't even bothered appearing for supper last night, leaving Deannie utterly relieved.

The incident in the cabin had shaken her deeply. Not so much removing cactus thorns from his delectable posterior but from kissing him. She had been hard-pressed to explain to herself the nature of the mysterious emotions his kisses generated.

Why did she go soft and melting inside every time she caught a glimpse of him riding across the field? Why did her heart hammer just a little harder when his voice caught her ear? Why did the guilt she'd been fighting so hard to suppress come swinging back with a vengeance, her conscience nagging her day and night to reconsider her plan to trick Brodie Trueblood into marriage?

Deannie pondered these questions as she waited in the back seat of Brodie's extended-cab pickup truck while Buster and Angel crawled all over her lap. The children chattered excitedly and bounced up and down on the cushions.

"I get to hold him first," Buster announced asserting his authority. "'Cause I'm the big brother."

"Nuh-uh." Angel thrust her bottom lip out in a pout. "I getta hold him first."

"Deannie," Buster insisted. "Tell her she's too little to hold the baby."

"Am not!" Angel shrieked and dove at her brother with her fists flailing.

"Stop it, you two," Deannie commanded, grabbing each child by the back of the collar and forcing them to sit down. "Do you want your mother to find you fighting?"

"No, ma'am," Buster said solemnly.

"No, 'am," Angel echoed.

"Good. Then settle down."

Deannie glanced at the hospital entrance, and what she saw had her blood running cold. There, stalking the sidewalk, was Brodie's old housekeeper, Matilda Jennings.

The minute the gray-haired woman spotted the pickup, she came marching over.

"There's 'Tilda," Buster said.

"Me don't like her," Angel whimpered.

Matilda, her sourpuss face drawn down into a frown, rapped on the window. Reluctantly, Deannie rolled it down.

"Well, well, well, if it isn't little Miss Priss."

Deannie's heart stuttered in her chest. Willing her expression to remain impassive, she met Matilda's stare. "What do you want?" she asked curtly.

"I know you're up to no good." Matilda shook a finger under Deannie's nose. "And I'm gonna keep after you until I figure out what game you're playing. Brodie Trueblood might be a trusting fool, but I ain't."

"Excuse me." Deannie said, her stomach roiling. "I don't have to listen to this." She leaned over and started to roll the window back up.

"Not so fast." Matilda slapped her palm against the window frame. "I'm not done with you yet, missy."

"What do you want?" Deannie demanded, narrowing her eyes. The woman knew nothing, otherwise she would already have gone to Brodie with her suspicions

Matilda's eyes gleamed. "I want in on the action."

"There is no 'action.'"

"Don't yank my chain, honey. You're angling to get that man to marry you so you can run herd over Willow Creek. If I was twenty years younger I'd be pulling the same stunt myself."

Fear jelled in Deannie's veins but she wasn't about to let the woman see her sweat. "Don't be absurd. I have no interest in Willow Creek Ranch or Brodie Trueblood, for that matter."

"Lie through your teeth all you want, girlie, I learned

the real scoop from some of those fellas you played poker with at the Lonesome Dove. Just remember, I'm on to you, and I intend on either getting my job back or making a pile of money off you."

"Are you threatening me, Mrs. Jennings?" Deannie asked coldly. She put on a brave front, but her insides were liquid terror. "Last time I checked, blackmail was against the law."

"So's defrauding people."

"I haven't defrauded anyone. If you'll please take your hand off the door, I'd like to roll up the window."

"You haven't seen the last of me," Matilda warned. "I'll be in touch." With that, the middle-aged woman strolled away leaving Deannie quaking all over. What if Matilda made good her threats and dug around until she found out Deannie was really Deanna Hollis?

"Look," Buster said. "There's Mama."

"Where?" Angel shouted.

Sucking in wind, Deannie stared at Brodie coming down the walkway, carrying a bundle wrapped in blue. The smiling dark-haired woman seated in a wheelchair at his side was being wheeled along by an attendant.

When they reached the vehicle parking in the passenger loading zone, Brodie opened the right side door, and the attendant helped Patsy Ann inside. When she was seated, Brodie gently handed her the tiny bundle.

For once, Angel and Buster were totally silent. Their eyes loomed wide in their faces, and their mouths hung open as they leaned over the seat to view the newest Trueblood.

Deannie, still shaken from her encounter with the housekeeper, kept her hands in her lap and her eyes averted. Everything had changed. Before Matilda's revelation, Deannie had envisioned plenty of time to woo Brodie. Suddenly, the whole plan had accelerated. She could no longer afford the luxury of waiting. She had to secure Brodie's marriage proposal and the sooner the better.

"This is my brother?" Buster asked his mother, awe apparent in his voice.

"Yes, honey," Patsy Ann turned to smile at her oldest child and caught a glimpse of Deannie. She winked. "Hi, I'm Patsy Ann and I'm assuming you're Deannie. Brodie's told me so much about you. He says you're a real whiz with the kids."

It was impossible not to return Patsy Ann's engaging grin. In spite of herself and the anxiety crawling through her stomach, Deannie smiled. "I like a challenge."

"Oh." Patsy Ann chuckled. "I see you do know my children."

"Kisses, Mommie," Angel insisted, puckering her lips and leaning over the seat to receive her request.

"Me, too," Buster said, not one to be left out.

Brodie got in and started the engine. Helplessly, Deannie stared at him, her gaze taking in the firm, clean lines of his broad shoulders and his unyielding posture. He tugged his hat lower over his forehead as if attempting to escape her perusal.

"Anyone want to see the baby?" Patsy Ann asked, once the round of kisses were completed.

"Oh, yes, Mommy, please." Angel clapped her hands and Patsy Ann unwrapped the wriggly little package in her lap.

Buster closed one eye and assessed his baby brother thoughtfully. "He's awfully small, Mama. You sure we shouldn't throw him back and wait till he's bigger."

Laughter at Buster's statement filled the cab. Brodie's chuckle was the deepest, longest. Watching Patsy Ann and her children, Deannie experienced a strange stab of jealousy.

We'll never bring our baby home from the hospital like this, Brodie and me.

That sad, desolate thought floated through her mind. But why should she care? All she wanted was Willow Creek Ranch. Not a man, and certainly not a passel of rowdy children. Deannie swallowed the lump in her throat and turned her eyes from the happy family.

No, she reminded herself, not entirely happy. There was Kenny living in exile and Patsy Ann perched on the verge of divorce with three small children to support.

The rest of the drive passed quickly as Angel and Buster oohed and aahed over the new addition. Deanna glanced up once to catch Brodie studying her in the rearview mirror, but when he realized she'd seen him, he pretended to be observing traffic.

When they reached the ranch, Brodie assisted Patsy Ann and the baby inside while Deannie corralled the two older kids.

"Me got the prettiest baby in the whole world," Angel cooed, clinging to Deannie's hand and skipping along beside her.

"Yes, you do," Deannie agreed. Darn. There it was again. That deep pang of something very important missing from her life.

They entered the house to find Patsy Ann, who had changed out of her street clothes. She and the baby were sitting on the couch with Brodie nowhere in sight. Angel and Buster crowded in on either side of their mother, both talking at once.

Patsy Ann cradled the baby in the curve of her arm, a Madonna smile on her lips. Wearing a hand-embroidered pink bed jacket over a matching nightgown, she positively glowed with the miracle of bringing another life into the world.

Deannie recalled Kenny saying he'd bought that bed jacket for his wife. Obviously, somewhere on the other side of his ornery Trueblood genes, Kenny wasn't such a bad guy.

Could Brodie actually reach his brother and help him to quit drinking? Deannie nibbled her bottom lip in thought.

She certainly hoped so; as long as Patsy Ann and the kids were living at Willow Creek, it would be much harder to take their home away from them. Unlike Rafe, Deannie found the idea of putting children onto the streets repugnant.

Deannie would start working on Patsy Ann to convince her to give her husband a second chance. Also, helping repair a family might go a long way in assuaging her own guilt over deceiving Brodie.

Then there was Matilda and her not-so-idle intimidations. But what could she do about the situation? Best to put it out of her mind for now and concentrate on the things she could control.

"Is there anything I can get for you?" Deannie asked.

"No, thank you," Patsy Ann smiled. "I'm fine for now."

"The new baby is very handsome."

"Would you like to hold him while I cuddle these two?" Deannie laid a hand on her chest. "Me?"

"Sure." Pasty Ann extended the baby toward her.

"B-but I've never held a baby before," Deannie stammered.

"Nothing to it. Just support his head like this. See?"

"What if I drop him?" She whispered, drawing closer.

"You won't."

Tentatively, Deannie reached out and took the newborn infant from his mother's arms. He opened his eyes and peered at her in a fuzzy, unfocused manner.

A feeling of reverence settled over Deannie as she stared at his tiny hands. His face was slightly red and his features scrunchy, but Phillip Brodie was the most adorable thing she had ever seen.

"It's amazing," she said, not knowing what else to say.

"I know." A satisfied smile extended to Patsy Ann's warm brown eyes. "Just wait until you have your own."

Deannie shook her head. "I doubt if I'll ever have children."

Patsy Ann's mouth formed a circle of concern. "Surely you're not serious."

"The world's a pretty rough place, why bring a child into it."

"Because babies are the only hope we have of redeeming the future," Patsy Ann said quietly.

"It's too bad," Deannie replied, "that his father isn't here to enjoy the moment."

Her statement completely obliterated the joy from Patsy Ann's face. "Yes," she said tightly, casting glances at the other two children snuggling against her. "It is bad when their father won't grow up and assume responsibility for his family."

"I'm sorry," Deannie apologized, "if I spoke out of turn."

"You didn't say anything that wasn't true."

"What's not true?" Buster perked up.

"Nothing, darling. Why don't you take your sister and run upstairs and get a diaper for the baby. Can you do that for Mommy?"

"You bet I can." In an instant Buster was on his feet. "Come on, Angel, let's go."

Angel, for once in an acquiescent mood, took her brother's hand and followed him upstairs.

"Have a seat." Patsy Ann patted the couch cushion beside her. "Even though he's tiny it doesn't take long for him to get heavy."

Deannie sank down next to her. The baby yawned widely and rubbed at his face with his small fists.

"I'm going to have to watch what I say about Kenny in front of the kids. Little pitchers have big ears."

"If you don't want to talk about it, I understand. Really, it's none of my business," Deannie replied, surprised at how frank and open Patsy Ann was about the subject. "But Brodie told me you and Kenny were getting divorced, and

I couldn't help but think that was such a shame. You with a new baby and all.''

Patsy Ann swallowed hard, and Deannie could tell she was fighting back tears. "Actually, it's good to have someone to talk to. Most of my family lives in Midland, and though we've only just met, I think you and I are going to be good friends.''

"You do?''

Patsy Ann nodded. "I have a feeling you're going to be around here for a while. Brodie likes you a lot.''

"Really?'' Deannie ducked her head.

"He speaks very highly of you.''

"I like him, too.''

"He's a good man. Not at all like his father and my soon-to-be-ex-husband.''

"What do you mean?'' Deannie asked, knowing exactly what Patsy Ann meant. She was far too familiar with the negative characteristics of the Trueblood clan.

Patsy Ann sighed. "Rafe, their dad, was the most engaging man, he could charm a raccoon out of a tree. But he was real polecat. He drank and gambled and chased women. Both Brodie and Kenny believe his behavior is what drove their mother to an early grave.''

"How awful.''

"Did Brodie tell you how Rafe managed to get hold of a place like Willow Creek?''

Deannie shook her head.

"He won it. Gambling. Do you know what else he did?''

"No,'' Deannie said in a quiet whisper, the sleeping baby deadweight in her arm.

"He threw the man out on the street in the middle of the night. Him and his seven-year-old daughter.'' Patsy Ann clicked her tongue. "What kind of person does such a heartless thing?''

Deannie froze at Patsy Ann's words. What kind of person indeed?

"Of course I didn't know Rafe back then. Apparently he mellowed a lot by the time I came on the scene. You couldn't help but like him, he was so friendly, but you knew never to trust him with your money."

"I don't even see how you could like such a man." Deannie's tone was frosty. The idea that Rafe had any redeemable qualities whatsoever was an affront to her sensibilities.

"Oh, you know," Patsy Ann waved a hand. "Rafe was a big flirt. Unfortunately, Kenny took after him. He swept me off my feet. I was young. He was a motorcycle-riding bad boy. So exciting. By the time I realized that Kenny was never going to grow up, I was madly in love with him and two-months pregnant with Buster."

Deannie said nothing. What could she say?

"Things were really pretty good in the beginning. Kenny made a big effort to settle down. He took a job in the oil fields. We rented a little two-bedroom house on Pinion Street. Sure, Kenny went out on Friday nights with his buddies, but I didn't mind. He was bringing home good money and we had everything we needed."

"So what happened?"

Patsy Ann sighed and toyed with a loose thread on her bed jacket. "After Angel was born, Kenny got laid off."

Deannie made sympathetic noises.

"He came to work for Brodie here at the ranch. But Kenny wanted to be the boss, and of course Willow Creek is Brodie's baby. He's made this ranch what it is today. Not Rafe, not Kenny."

And not my father. "Must have been hard for all of you."

"Brodie fired Kenny for coming to work drunk."

"Ouch."

"He did offer to let us live here, but Kenny wouldn't hear of it. That's when things started getting bad. Kenny would hang out at the Lonesome Dove drinking and gambling away our savings. If I said anything to him, he would fly into a rage and call me a nagging shrew." Patsy's bottom lip trembled.

"You don't have to say any more." Deannie patted the other woman's knee.

"I think I need to talk about it. To try and figure out what went wrong. I will say one thing for Kenny, I know he never cheated on me. At least I haven't had to bear *that* cross, as well." Patsy Ann laced her fingers together and was silent for a moment before she continued.

"Then Rafe died almost three weeks ago, and the stuff really hit the fan."

"What do you mean?"

"Rafe had been sick with liver failure for several months. We all knew it was getting near the end. I think Kenny had been counting on an inheritance to bail us out."

Deannie waited quietly.

"Turns out Rafe left everything to Brodie. Nobody was more shocked than Kenny. He and Rafe had been two of a kind. They partied together, hung out together, understood each other. If anything, I imagine Kenny thought he'd inherit Willow Creek over Brodie."

The clock on the mantel ticked loudly in the still room. Only the sound of the baby's soft breathing disrupted the silence.

"Kenny went off the deep end. We had a terrible fight, and I left him. Brodie invited me to stay here until I can figure out what I want to do."

"And you've decided to divorce Kenny."

"Deannie, what else can I do? I refuse to live the way Melinda Trueblood lived all those years, loving a man who was so selfish he thought only of his own earthly pleasures. I might have made a few mistakes in my life, but I'm not a total fool."

Deannie squeezed Patsy Ann's hands. "I'm so sorry."

Patsy Ann wiped an errant tear from her eye. "It's hard, you know. Dealing with all this when you're pregnant."

"I can only imagine." Deannie shook her head again. "Do you think you could give him another chance?" She could not believe she was taking the side of a Trueblood.

"I still love Kenny. But I simply cannot take him back until he proves he's willing and able to change for good. I've had enough. There's only so much a woman can be expected to accept."

"Hey, Mama, we couldn't finded no diapers," Angel said, bouncing down the stairs ahead of her brother.

Buster was scratching his head and looking puzzled.

"What's the matter, son?" Patsy Ann said, quickly drying her tears and pasting a smile on her face.

"How come Uncle Brodie's packing a suitcase?" Buster asked.

Patsy Ann arched an eyebrow and looked at Deannie.

Deannie shrugged her shoulders in surprise.

Brodie appeared at the top of the stairs, two suitcases clutched in his hands.

"What's happening?" Patsy Ann demanded, staring at her brother-in-law.

"Uh...well...I thought I'd give you ladies the run of the house," he replied.

"What do you mean?" Patsy Ann said. "Where are you going?"

Brodie carefully avoided Deannie's gaze. "With a new baby in the house I thought you might need your space," he told Patsy Ann. "So I figured I'd hole up in the old log cabin for a few weeks."

"That's absurd, I'm not turning you out of your house."

"Please, Patsy Ann, it's as much your house as it is mine," he insisted.

"Brodie..."

"Come on, Patsy Ann, I just need a little privacy."

Deannie peeked at Brodie from behind lowered lashes.

She knew exactly why Brodie was moving into that cabin. It had nothing to do with Patsy Ann and the kids and everything to do with her.

Brodie headed out the door. Deannie felt a sudden urge to intercept him to find out what was going on inside his head. Gently, she eased the baby back into Patsy Ann's arms and followed Brodie outside.

"What's this all about?" she asked, sinking her hands on her hips as he tossed his suitcases into the bed of the pickup truck.

He avoided looking at her. "Kenny needs me to stay him on the straight and narrow. Please don't tell Patsy Ann where he's at."

"That's not the real reason you're running away," she insisted.

Brodie climbed into the cab and slammed the door shut. Turning the key, he revved the engine. "What do you want me to say, Deannie?" he spoke at last. "That after what happened yesterday I can't trust myself around you? Is that what you want to hear?"

"Is it the truth?"

He snorted and glared out the dusty windshield. "What do you think?"

A thrill hurdled through her. Things were changing between them, shifting and evolving into a potent stew of emotions neither could understand or control.

"Would you like me to leave Willow Creek?" she asked.

"No." His response was swift and unequivocal. "You need a place to stay, and Patsy Ann needs someone to help her. She's going to be upset when Kenny doesn't come around for a while."

"What about you, Brodie Trueblood? What do you need?"

He met her eyes at last. "I need you, Deannie McCellan, so badly I can taste it. That's why I can't stay in the same house with you. We don't know enough about each other, and I'd hate for either you or me to suffer third-degree burns from this fire burning between us.''

The certainty of his conviction startled her. She watched as he threw the truck into gear and backed out of the driveway. Had she broken through his carefully constructed defenses? Had she gotten to him? Her heart pitched at the concept. The answer it seemed, was yes.

Only trouble was, he'd gotten to her, too!

Chapter Nine

Seeing Deannie holding the baby had done something strange and illogical to Brodie's brain. She appeared so sweet, so maternal that for one crazy moment he'd pretended she was holding their baby.

Whoa, Trueblood, slow it way down.

It was a damn good thing he'd already made up his mind to move into the cabin with Kenny. He hadn't seen any other way of dealing with his attraction to Deannie McCellan. The minute he was around her he wanted to scoop her into his arms, take her into his bedroom and make love to her until the sun came up.

It was too soon in their tenuous relationship for him to be taking the kind of steps his heart urged him to take. Besides, a few weeks in Kenny's company might do them both a world of good. Perhaps they could take a stab at repairing the rift that had begun so long ago when Kenny had sided with Rafe, and Brodie had staunchly supported their mother.

Driving to the cabin, Brodie tried his best to concentrate on the ranch and the work that needed doing, but his imagination kept returning to that living room, his mind's eye clearly focused on Deannie McCellan cradling his newborn nephew against her breasts.

He wanted to be cradled there, Brodie realized. He ached to wake up next to her every morning, to fall asleep by her side every night. He longed to give his emotions free rein, but he was scared. Terrified, in fact, that she would go back to her old way of life, which included drinking and gambling. What would he do if he allowed himself to fall in love with her, then discovered she was a female Rafe, out for only herself and a good time? As much as he might long to throw caution to the wind and take a chance, he simply couldn't. Not until he knew what secrets Deannie kept shuttered behind those ice blue eyes.

And he had enough trouble right now helping Kenny rehabilitate himself; he needed no added personal burdens.

Only time would tell if Deannie McCellan was serious in her efforts to leave her past behind, and he could not afford the dangers inherent in whiling away the days under the same roof with her.

Killing the engine outside the log cabin, Brodie waved a hand to Kenny, who was busy putting the screen door back on its hinges.

"Hey, little brother." Kenny stopped working, ran the back of his hand across his forehead and approached the truck. "How's Patsy Ann?"

"She's fine."

"And the baby?"

"He's good." Brodie slammed the door and retrieved his suitcases from the truck bed.

"Don't tell me you're moving in."

"Yeah. I am."

"That's not fair, Brodie," Kenny protested, sinking his hands on his hips. "You don't have to baby-sit me. I promised I was finished with drinking for good, and I mean it.

Losing my wife brought me to my senses. I don't intend to end up like the old man."

"For once, Kenny, this isn't about you."

"What are you talking about?"

"I need somewhere to stay."

Kenny whistled long and low. "It's that redhead, isn't it."

Brodie didn't answer.

"It is! I can't believe it. You're in love with her."

"I'm not in love with her," Brodie denied, but his pulse sped up at the concept.

"I'll be damned. I never thought ol' stony-hearted Brodie would fall in love," Kenny teased.

"What's that supposed to mean?"

"What do you think it means, little brother? When have you ever been in love with anyone but your mama?"

Brodie rounded on his brother. "You leave Mama out of this. You know I've always been too busy running this ranch to have time for women. Unlike some people I could name."

Kenny raised both palms. "Hey, I'm not looking for a fight."

"Then stop picking one."

"Sure *you* don't have a hangover?"

"You know I don't drink," Brodie snapped.

"Does this have anything to do with yesterday when me and the kids caught you with your pants down?"

"I told you what happened!" Brodie glared. "There's nothing going on between me and Deannie McCellan."

"Yeah, right, cactus in the backside. A likely story."

Brodie started to rise to the bait until he realized Kenny was grinning, just itching to continue the argument. He refused to give his brother the satisfaction.

"Why are you giving me a hard time? You're the one who's in the hot seat." He slung his arm over Kenny's shoulder.

Grumbling good naturedly, Kenny followed him into the cabin. A joyful feeling lifted Brodie's spirits. He couldn't remember when he'd felt so free, so optimistic. Things seemed to be falling into place at last. His brother had finally recognized his problems and was seeking help. His father had bequeathed him a thriving ranch, and the most beautiful woman in the world was living in his house. A woman who, the good Lord willing, might someday concede to become his bride. Brodie Trueblood was perched on the verge of having his every dream fulfilled at last. He needed a little patience and a little perseverance but that was okay.

He possessed all the time in the world.

May flowed into June, then June spilled over into July. The temperature flared hotter, the grass burned drier. Peaches clinging to the trees in the backyard went from hard green knots to lush ripe fruit that fell readily into waiting palms. Patsy Ann's baby grew fat and happy with frequent feedings and constant attention. But with each passing day, Deannie's heart sank heavier.

Six weeks had elapsed since she had come home to Willow Creek Ranch. Six weeks spent lying, conniving and manipulating. Six weeks of dodging guilt and battling fear of discovery. Six of the most miserable weeks of her life.

Oh, she was contented enough with her day-to-day existence. Chasing after Buster and Angel kept her physically occupied. She fed them, bathed them, dressed them. She read stories and took them on pony rides. She donned a swimming suit and splashed with the children in the lawn sprinkler. She braided Angel's hair and fussed over Buster when he made a fist and proudly showed her his "muscles."

But mentally, emotionally, she was a wreck. Coming home had not brought the peace of mind she had always assumed it would bring. No matter how hard she tried,

Deannie could not erase Brodie Trueblood from her mind. He'd burrowed under her skin but good, and the thought that she was going to break his heart ate at her day and night.

He trusted her when he shouldn't. He'd opened his home to her. He'd given her a job and treated her just like family.

And she repaid him with deception.

Brodie's self-imposed exile in the cabin had only increased Deannie's desire for him. He no longer took his meals in the dining room with the ranch hands, preferring instead to dine with Kenny. In fact, he rarely came to the house at all. Occasionally, Deannie would catch sight of him from the window as he helped with the cattle or rode Ranger across the pasture. She lived for those brief sightings and counted the long hours until she saw him again.

She'd gone to the cabin once to visit him, but he'd told her it was best if she stayed away, at least until Kenny was ready to reveal his new persona to Patsy Ann. Not knowing what else to do, Deannie had agreed and kept her distance, even though time was running out. She couldn't wait forever. Sooner or later, Matilda Jennings was bound to discover her real identity, then the jig would be up.

With each passing day, tension mounted as Deannie struggled to deal with her internal dilemma and the loneliness Brodie's absence created.

Deannie was reminded of that old musical *Seven Brides for Seven Brothers* where the naughty menfolk had been banished to the barn for the winter. It felt like that, so close to Brodie and yet so far. She and Patsy Ann living in the big rambling farmhouse with the kids, with Kenny and Brodie isolated in the log cabin, miles from the ranch's main hub.

"Penny for your thought." Patsy Ann's voice cracked through her barrier.

"Huh?"

Deannie looked up from where they sat shelling peas at

the kitchen table. The smell of brisket roasting in the smoker on the back patio wafted in through the open window. The baby was sleeping in his bassinet beside them, while Angel and Buster sat on the floor making Fourth of July decorations with construction paper, glitter and paste.

"You've been so far away lately," Patsy Ann prodded. "Is there anything you'd like to talk about?"

"No," Deannie murmured.

"I wish Kenny would call," Patsy Ann fretted. "I can't believe he hasn't even come by to see the baby."

"Maybe he found a job out of town," Deannie ventured, trying to cast Patsy Ann's husband in a positive light.

"Not very likely. He's probably living at the Lonesome Dove. Deannie, I know Kenny has his faults but I always though he cared about me and the kids." Patsy Ann sniffled.

"Don't give up hope." She leaned over to pat the other woman's hand. "Maybe your ultimatum scared him. Anyone can change if they want it badly enough."

Even though it hurt keeping Patsy Ann in the dark, Deannie was glad she and Brodie had sworn all the ranch hands to secrecy. This way Patsy Ann would be pleasantly surprised by Kenny's transformation.

Patsy Ann pressed the hem of her apron against her eyes to stay the tears. "Rafe Trueblood's son? You've got to be kidding."

Deannie glanced out the window and spied Brodie striding up the walk. Joy leaped in her heart. Her eyes imbibed him like a dieter at a feast. Oh! He was so handsome with his straw work hat clutched tentatively in his hands. Her arms ached to hold him, her lips longed to kiss him.

He knocked at the back door before opening it and stepping over the threshold. "Hi!" He greeted everyone with a wide smile, but his gaze slid over Deannie as if reluctant to match her stare.

"Hey, stranger," Patsy Ann said. "Long time no see. Whatcha been up to?"

"Getting that cabin straightened up a bit."

"When are you going to move back in here?" his sister-in-law asked. "It's plumb ridiculous you hiding out in that cabin."

"Maybe soon." He peeked at Deannie, then quickly looked away.

"Any word from Kenny?" Patsy Ann asked, rolling her hands into fists.

"Actually, that's what I came in to tell you."

Patsy Ann's face paled and she laid a hand over her heart. "Is anything wrong? Kenny's not hurt is he?"

"Kenny's fine, but he'd like your permission to spend the holiday with you and the kids."

"Since when did Kenny Trueblood ever need my permission to do anything?"

"Since now."

Everyone looked over to see Kenny standing on the porch, a worried expression on his face.

"Daddy!" Buster and Angel cried in unison and flung themselves at the door.

"Kenny?" Patsy Ann rose to her feet, her palm pressed flat against her throat.

"Hello, Patsy Ann," Kenny said, his voice thick with emotion. He let himself in through the back door and scooped up a child in each arm. He kissed his children soundly on the tops of their heads, all the while keeping his eyes trained on his wife's face.

Something inside Deannie cracked. Another chunk of her defenses broke right off, leaving her vulnerable and exposed. How had she gotten so involved in the daily lives of these people? She'd never meant to know them on a personal basis. For fifteen years one thought had dominated her mind—win back Willow Creek.

But she'd discovered things were simply not that easy.

From the very beginning, when she had stepped into the Lonesome Dove and discovered Rafe Trueblood was dead, her plans had begun to unravel, forcing Deannie to question her goals and reexamine her motives. Was recovering her home worth hurting the people she'd come to care about so deeply? How much was she willing to sacrifice for revenge, and what price was too high?

Deannie watched the scene unfolding between husband and wife, her fingers laced together, her back stiff with tension.

"Where have you been?" Patsy Ann asked Kenny, her whole body trembling.

"Living in the cabin with Brodie."

"Why didn't you come to see us?" Pasty Ann asked.

"I was afraid you didn't want me around." Kenny hung his head. "I haven't been much of a husband lately."

"We were worried about you," his wife replied huskily.

"I got something to tell you, Patsy Ann." Tears misted Kenny's eyes.

"Yes?" She clutched her hands together and stepped toward him. Neither appeared to notice the children. They had eyes only for each other.

"I've been so wrong."

"What are you saying?"

"Brodie's helped me see the light."

"Deannie's been talking to me, too. I'd forgotten how blessed I am to have a family." Patsy Ann smiled gratefully at her.

"Honey, you were one hundred percent in the right. You've done nothing wrong."

"That's not true, Kenny. I nagged, I harangued, I made you feel like less of a man."

"If you hadn't threatened to divorce me, I might never have straightened up my act, but I swear to you I haven't touched a drop of liquor in six weeks. I've been going to

AA meetings. I got a job working for Hubert Barnes at the feed store. It's not much, but it's a start.''

"Oh, Kenny," Patsy Ann said.

He raised a palm. "Let me finish. Brodie wants to give us our half of the ranch. We can build our home on the back acreage. He's also going to give us a hundred head of cattle to start our own herd.''

"Is it true?" she whispered. "Did you give up your bad habits for me and the kids?"

"Yeah, baby. Can you ever forgive me?" Kenny dropped to his knees and reached out for his wife. "I love you, Patsy Ann, I always have and I always will.''

"I love you, too, Kenny Trueblood. From the moment you came driving up to my dorm room at Texas Tech. on that bad-boy motorcycle of yours," Patsy Ann sobbed, and dissolved into her husband's waiting arms.

No matter what problems Patsy Ann and Kenny faced, their love for each other was evident in their voices, the way they held each other, the lingering looks they exchanged. Deannie's heart welled in her chest. Would anyone ever love her like that? Was there a man who could forgive all her faults and overlook her sins? She cast a glance at Brodie and her breath snagged.

He studied her intently. His dark eyes narrowed and grew shiny against the sunlight flooding in through the window.

They locked gazes, and time seemed suspended. She could never forget this moment. It would hang in her brain whenever she conjured up images of the Fourth of July. No longer would firecrackers and barbecue and watermelon dominate her memories of Independence Day. Instead, Deanna Rene Hollis would always remember the date as the exact instant when she realized she had done the unthinkable and fallen in love with Brodie Trueblood.

Staring into Deannie's eyes, Brodie felt as if he'd finally found what he'd been searching for his entire life—someone to love. Perhaps it was emotions exacerbated by Kenny and Patsy Ann's tearful reunion, but that knowledge didn't change the feelings whipping and diving inside him as Deannie McCellan's ice blue gaze merged with his in a head-on collision of the heart.

"I better go check the brisket," Deannie said, clearing her throat and breaking their connection. Patsy Ann and Kenny, still locked in their embrace, were oblivious.

"How 'bout me and the kids giving you a hand," Brodie offered, anxious to give his brother time alone with his wife. If truth be told, he was just as anxious to be alone with Deannie, but that wasn't about to happen with Buster and Angel clinging to his hands.

"Come on, troops," Deannie sang out, picking up a pot holder and a pair of tongs on her way through the kitchen.

A kid tucked in the crook of each elbow, Brodie followed her outside, his gaze riveted to the provocative motions of Deannie's backside. Her thick red mane swished below her shoulders causing a riot inside his pants. Brodie gulped. Six weeks without her had been too long.

Sure, he'd seen her. He'd watched her from his position astride Ranger as she went about her daily chores. He'd even talked to her a time or two over the backyard fence while she played with the children. But it had been six long weeks since he'd been within touching distance. His fingers ached to skim her soft skin, his lips hungered to taste her sweet mouth, his nose twitched to be buried against that long pale neck and inhale her glorious magnolia scent.

"Why don't you kids get down and go swing?" Brodie pointed to the swing set. "While I help Aunt Deannie with the food."

Aunt Deannie.

Where had that come from? She hadn't missed the slip of his tongue. Her shoulders stiffened, and she made a pointed effort to keep her eyes focused on the barbecue grill.

She lifted the lid, giving him a potent dose of smoked brisket. Brodie's mouth watered, but not from the want of food.

"That was really wonderful what you did for Kenny and Patsy Ann," she said, studiously flipping the meat.

"Kenny's my brother. Nothing makes me happier than to have peace in the family at last. We both realized my father is the one who kept our rivalry stirred up." Was it his imagination or did Deannie's shoulders just grow stiffer? "With Rafe gone, we did a lot of talking and got a lot of hard feelings out of the way."

"That's nice," she murmured.

"Out there in the cabin, I had a lot of time to think."

"Oh? What about?"

Darn it, he wished she would look at him. "Us."

"Us?" she echoed.

Was that fear he detected in her voice? Tentatively he reached over and cupped her chin in his palm. She kept her lashes lowered, refusing to let him in.

"You know," he said hoarsely. "Us. As in you and me."

"Brodie...I..."

"I know I said we'd wait three months before we discussed changing our relationship, but these past six weeks without you have been pure torture. I missed you, Deannie, more than you can know."

Please, he thought, *please let her give us a chance.*

But she said nothing. Just waited with the tongs outstretched in her hands.

"Look at me."

Her lashes fluttered and she gulped. Briefly her eyes met his, but then she quickly glanced away again as if desperate to hide something. "I thought you had a lot of reservations about my past."

"I'm not saying we should jump into anything. I just wanted you to know I'm moving back into the house."

"Thanks for telling me." She pulled back. "Gotta tend to supper."

Reluctantly he let her go, confusion swamping him. Did she want him or not? The woman sent mixed messages, and he simply did not know how to read her. Was she hiding something? Were her secrets darker than gambling and hanging out in honky-tonks?

Brodie swallowed hard and realized it didn't matter. Whatever she'd done, whatever secrets she harbored, they would deal with it together. He would back off for now, but soon he would get her alone and they would have a long talk. For if he'd extracted one thing from the lessons Patsy Ann and Kenny had to offer, Brodie had learned true love could triumph over any obstacles.

She had to leave. As soon as possible. Before Brodie did what she'd been angling for him to do ever since she'd faked a broken-down car—ask her to marry him.

Because once he uttered those four little words, it would be all over. Deannie knew she didn't have the courage to say no. She had to get out before he made her an offer she couldn't refuse.

Looking over, she studied his profile in the gathering twilight, and her heart jerked. He was so handsome, so kind, so honest. She'd never anticipated a Trueblood possessing such qualities. But Brodie did. In spades.

If only she'd known! She would never have started this revenge campaign. Her dark motives had repercussions beyond her control. Repercussions that caused everyone lots of pain. In that respect, she was no different from Rafe Trueblood, putting her own agenda ahead of everything else.

Sorrow was her penance, losing both Willow Creek and Brodie's love. Sadness, remorse and regret melded into a tight ball in her throat. She'd made so many bad decisions. The honorable choice was to disappear from his life forever and spend the rest of *her* life trying to make amends for what she'd done.

They sat in lawn chairs on the back porch enjoying the lazy heat. Hummingbirds hovered near the feeder, drinking one last time before settling down for the night. The grass was damp from the sprinklers and issued an earthy odor.

After a hearty supper of sliced barbecue, potato salad, baked beans, corn on the cob and homemade peach ice cream, Kenny and Patsy Ann had taken the baby and disappeared upstairs arm in arm, leaving the other two children with Deannie and Brodie.

Angel sat in Deannie's lap, Buster in Brodie's. They had already had their baths and were dressed in pajamas. Cooter Gates had joined them, and he leisurely gnawed on the stem of an unlit pipe while they waited for Rory and the other ranch hands to orchestrate a fireworks display just beyond the chain-link fence.

Stars lit the edge of the sky as the sun slipped behind the horizon. Crickets chirped. Cattle lowed. Honeysuckle drifted on the air and mingled with the scent of charcoal.

Tears nudged against the back of Deannie's eyes. Angel leaned into her chest, and Deannie lightly kissed the top of her head. The child smelled of bubble bath and strawberry shampoo.

She would leave tonight after the kids were in bed, Deannie made up her mind, it was the only way.

"You folks ready?" Rory hollered from across the fence.

"Yes!" Angel and Buster squealed in unison.

Brodie chuckled. The happy sound filled Deannie's ears, twisting her already-raw emotions like the tightening of a screw.

Torture. Sitting here in the pleasant evening, anticipating fireworks, children clutched in their laps, they were the epitome of an ordinary couple on the Fourth of July. The illusion tormented her. Deep inside, this was what Deannie had longed her whole life to recover. Willow Creek. An intact family unit. An honorable man to love her.

Closing her eyes, she swallowed past her grief. She'd almost achieved her goal, but the victory was hollow. She couldn't accept it. She'd manipulated and finagled. She'd lied and deceived. Once Brodie knew the truth, he would no longer care about her.

Yes, everything she'd ever wanted was within her grasp but she could not close her fist and take it.

The explosion startled her. She jumped, jostling Angel into her chin and Deannie's eyes flew open just as the rocket flared into a starburst of bright colors.

"Wow," Buster exclaimed and clapped his hands.

The gunpowder odor, thick and metallic, invaded their nostrils. Rory torched another wick, and the second rocket followed the first into oblivion.

"Ah," Cooter Gates exclaimed. "I love the smell of the Fourth of July. It's nice having kids at the ranch again."

Deannie lightly caressed Angel's bare arm and strained to hear Cooter, who spoke softly and was sitting on the other side of Brodie.

Cooter stared unseeingly into the past, his pipe cupped in his palm. "Yep," he whispered. "I can still remember Gil Hollis's little girl laughing and squealing while I set off the fireworks."

Deannie froze, her heart thumping in her chest. Did Cooter suspect? All the more reason to leave Willow Creek before the old foreman's supposition was confirmed. She wanted to vanish without Brodie ever finding out how she'd planned to cheat him out of his home.

"I've got a headache," Deannie said, rubbing her temple. It wasn't a lie. "Could you put the children to bed for me?"

"You okay?" Brodie patted her hand.

The tenderness in his eyes, the concern in his voice had

her stomach rolling over. She did not deserve his kind consideration.

"I just need to lie down for a while."

"Sure, sure. Go on upstairs," Brodie assured her. "Come on, Angel, get in my lap."

Deannie transferred the girl to the crook of his arm and almost ran into the house, desperate to escape Brodie's compassionate perusal. She fled to her room, the tears she'd pushed back for so long now streaming down her cheeks in torrents.

Dropping to her knees, she dragged her duffel bag from under the bed, then began emptying out the dresser drawers and stuffing her things inside. She had to go. It would be far too easy to stay, to pretend she'd never had revenge on her mind. To let herself fall completely in love with Brodie Trueblood. To marry him, bear his children, stay with him for the rest of her life and carry her secret to her grave.

But how could she do such a thing? How could they ever build a life together with no real trust between them? How could she spend a lifetime deceiving the man she'd come to care about more than anything on the face of the earth? More even, than Willow Creek Ranch and the memory of her father's shame,

Packed and ready, she lay on the bed fully dressed and waited.

An hour passed. Outside, the fireworks continued. She heard the resounding bangs, the sizzles and pops. She saw the colored lights flare and dissipate through the thin lace curtains of her bedroom window. She smelled gunpowder and barbecue lingering on her skin and in her hair.

Deannie groaned and covered her head with the pillow, trying her best to shut out all sensory input.

At long last the noises stopped. She strained for the sounds of Brodie trooping up the stairs. She heard his boots against the wood and his murmured voice as he tucked the children into their beds. Then she heard him moving around outside her door.

She squeezed her eyes shut and held her breath.

The door creaked open slightly. She could feel him standing in the doorway staring at her.

"Good night, Deannie," he said softly, then pulled the door closed behind him.

She stayed another hour, listening to the old house settle. Finally, when she was convinced everyone was asleep, she slid off the bed, gathered her duffel, took a deep breath and edged from the room.

Night-lights lit the hallway. All the bedroom doors were closed. Satisfied she was alone, Deannie eased downstairs.

A floorboard creaked, and she caught her breath. Her pulse roared louder than an idling race car engine but she knew the noise resounded only in her guilty ears.

The trip through the quiet house seemed to take an eternity, her memory snagging at each step.

Here, on the stairs, where she and Brodie had assisted Kenny the night he'd come to them drunk and seeking help.

There, in the living room, where she had sat with Patsy Ann, holding the baby and listening to her friend's troubles.

In the kitchen, by the stove, where she had learned how to cook by preparing meals for the ranch hands.

And the dining room, where she and Brodie had shared their first meal together. She could taste the roast beef sandwiches he'd made with his own caring hands.

Fresh tears scorched her cheeks by the time she reached the back door. How she wanted to stay! To leave her sad past behind and embrace the future. But to do so would be to live a lie, and she simply could not go through with it.

Locking the back door behind her, she stepped out into the warm night air, her car keys clutched firmly in her hand. A half-moon hung in the sky, lighting her way across the drive.

She kept her head down, too heartbroken to look back.

"Deannie."

His voice snaked out of the darkness and wrapped around her. No. It couldn't be Brodie.

His boots crunched on the gravel. She didn't have to turn to know he had been sitting in the shadows on the front porch and was now standing behind her.

"Where are you going?" Brodie asked, the pain in his voice impossible to miss. "You were sneaking off in the middle of the night without saying goodbye?"

She stood like a statue, unable to move, unable to answer.

"Deannie." His hand closed over her upper arm, and he turned her to face him.

She met his somber gaze and all resistance left her body. How could she leave this man? She did not deserve him, but how she wanted him!

"Brodie...I..."

"Where were you going?" he repeated, his dark eyes shimmering with unexpressed emotion.

"It's for the best," she said.

His grip tightened. "What are you talking about? We've got something going on here, you and me. I've been trying to deny it for six weeks, but it won't go away. I learned not to fight this feeling, sweetheart. You've got to let go and let it unfold."

Deannie whistled in a breath. "I can't."

"I know you're scared. I know there's something from your past that's keeping you on the run but please, Deannie, don't shut me out. Give us a chance to work through your problems."

How tempting it would be to accept his generous offer! To fling herself into his arms and confess everything. But she knew once he discovered the truth, that she had planned and schemed her way into this proposal, that her dark motive had been to cheat him out of Willow Creek, the love shinning in his eyes would wither and die.

"You don't understand," she said.

"I think I do." His fingers rubbed her skin in a provocative circle. "You need more from me than empty promises of what might one day be. You need a commitment."

"Oh, Brodie." She opened her mouth to refute his claim, to tell him no, to beg him not to say what was on his mind, for she didn't possess the courage to refuse him to his face. But it was too late.

Brodie Trueblood took a deep breath and spoke the words that Deannie had been waiting to hear from the moment she stepped into his headlights on the roadside. The words that would offer her everything she'd ever wanted. The words she had no willpower to reject.

"I love you, Deannie McCellan. Will you marry me?"

Chapter Ten

Brodie waited at the altar. He wore sharply creased black denim jeans and brand-new black boots under a black tuxedo jacket and white shirt. The stiff collar closed tighter around his throat, seemingly cutting off his oxygen supply.

The pianist had played the wedding march three times. The guests were shifting in their seats, craning their necks and staring expectantly at the staircase.

Kenny, appearing nervous and uncomfortable, waited beside him. At the back of the room, Angel nibbled on a white rose petal plucked from her wicker basket, and Buster, a white satin pillow clutched between his fists, wriggled impatiently.

The minister, Bible open in his palms, cleared his throat and raised his eyebrows.

Brodie shot a look at Patsy Ann. She shrugged and telegraphed him a helpless expression.

Deannie's going to stand me up.

The thought flashed through his mind and sent a spiked stab angling through his gut. No. Not that. Anything but that.

A hush, similar to the guarded reverence reserved for funeral parlors, settled over the small crowd. The clock over the mantel ticked loudly, expectantly. Brodie felt himself pale. The room grew suddenly very hot as every eye in the place rested upon him.

"Perhaps," the minister whispered, "you should go check on the bride."

Nodding, Brodie moved on automatic pilot. He turned, walked past his friends and marched up the stairs, knowing full well he was the center of attention. Without even looking, he knew what he would find when he reached the bedroom he and Deannie were supposed to share as man and wife.

Still, the reality of that empty room slammed him like a sucker punch to the solar plexus.

The window hung open, the screen was missing and the curtain flapped in the breeze. The room smelled of her perfume. Like a fragrant magnolia in full bloom, but she was nowhere in sight.

"Deannie?" Brodie said, even though he knew there would be no sweet reply.

Why?

That word reverberated in his brain and he had no answer. *Why, Deannie, why? Don't you love me?*

He stepped to the window and stared out at the cars below. Her battered old sedan sat hemmed in by visitors' vehicles. If she'd run, she'd done it on foot.

His stomach burned, his chest squeezed, his pulse turned thready as a ribbon winding off a spool.

No.

He trod the carpet, pacing, fighting the fog enveloping his mind. His boot contacted with something.

An earring. Tiny, white, delicate.

Brodie dropped to his knees, scooped up the earring and cupped it in his hands. It looked so incongruous, that petite

white pearl drop contrasting painfully with his large cal-
lused palms.

He almost broke down at that moment. The hollow ache
deep inside his soul that had started as a boy when he could
never win his father's affections widened into a yawning
chasm. In Deannie, he'd thought he'd found what he'd lost
with his mother's death—someone to love him, truly, hon-
estly, unconditionally.

He'd obviously been mistaken.

What did her departure mean? Had she gotten cold feet?
Was she scared of marriage and commitment? Or had his
greatest fear come to pass—she had never really loved him.

No, he could not believe that. How many times since
they'd become engaged had she raised her lips and stood
on her tiptoes, a teasing smile on her face, as she eagerly
sought to join her mouth with his? How frequently had she
reached for his hand as they sat side by side watching television or rocking on the front porch? How often had she
whispered "I love you"? Dozens? Hundreds? More?

Crouching beside the open window, Brodie ran a hand
through his hair and tried to think. There had to be an
explanation. Deannie wouldn't change her mind so quickly,
so dramatically without a damned good reason.

But what could justify her abandonment?

He recalled that night he'd asked her to be his bride. The
memory rose bittersweet and prophetic in his mind. He
should have known something was very wrong, something
that lurked deep within her psyche. She had been trying to
leave him even then.

When he'd spied her sneaking out to her car, duffel bag
in her hand, his spirits had sunk to his feet. Without thinking, without planning, without rehearsing his words, he'd
intercepted Deannie.

She had accepted his proposal willingly, throwing herself
into his arms with unbridled emotion. At that moment, any
doubts he'd harbored about their relationship had vanished

completely. He no longer feared that she wanted him just for his ranch and his money, or that she would fall back into her old ways and return to gambling. When he'd crushed her to his chest, felt her heart beating against his, he hadn't faltered. Asking her to marry him had come as easily as breathing.

And the ensuing weeks before the wedding had been pure heaven. They'd been so close. Laughing, talking, sharing, spending every free moment together. The single area that caused him concern was Deannie's continued reluctance to discuss her past. Every time he mentioned his childhood and encouraged her to open up about hers, she skirted the issue by changing the subject or giving him one-word replies. Since she'd otherwise been cheerful and bubbly, he'd dropped the issue, but now he wished he'd insisted on full disclosure, for something told him her current actions had everything to do with her unfortunate past.

"Brodie?" Kenny stood in the doorway, his hands clasped together. "Are you okay, little brother?"

"She's gone," Brodie replied, the hard little pearl earring cold in his fist. "Deannie ran out on me."

Kenny walked over and clapped a hand on his shoulder. "I'm sorry. I would have bet anything she was truly in love with you."

Brodie swallowed hard. "The hell of it is, I don't even know why she stood me up. I thought we were so happy. These past few months had been paradise. We never fought. We got along great. I guess I should have known it was too good to be true."

"I don't know what to say."

"I've got to find her." Brodie rose to his feet. "She couldn't have gotten far. Her car's still here."

"What about your truck?"

Brodie peered out the window, spotted his pickup parked under the car port where he'd left it. "No. There's the truck."

"You think she just took off walking?"

"I don't know what to think. Maybe she's hiding right here in the house, waiting for everyone to leave." That was a chilling thought. Deannie might even be skulking in the closet or under the bed.

"Nah, screen's on the ground, there's boot prints in the dirt. Deannie jumped out this window," Kenny observed, sticking his head out the window.

The image wrenched—Deannie, so desperate to get away from him that she would leap from a second-story bedroom in her wedding gown.

"Hey, didn't you leave Ranger saddled in the corral?" Kenny commented.

Brodie nodded. "I think so."

"Well I hate to alarm you, but he's gone."

Missing, just like Deannie.

"You think she left on the horse?" Brodie asked his brother.

"Yep."

"What's going on?" Patsy Ann stood in the doorway. "The crowd's getting restless. Where's Deannie?"

"Gone," Brodie said sadly.

Patsy Ann frowned and tapped the face of her watch. "I talked to her not fifteen minutes ago. Where could she be?"

Brodie pivoted on his heels to face his sister-in-law. "How did she act? What did she say?"

"She acted nervous, like all brides. I tried to reassure her," Patsy Ann said. "I told her love was worth all the ups and downs."

She looked at her husband with adoring eyes. Kenny walked over and slipped his arm around her waist.

"I've got to find her," Brodie said. "If she's riding Ranger, she's bound to be on the ranch, she couldn't risk being spotted by heading down the road into town."

Brodie was halfway down the stairs before he remembered he had a roomful of guests assembled. All eyes turned his way. Brodie took a deep breath. He didn't have time to be chagrined or embarrassed. He had to find Deannie before she disappeared from his life forever. The very idea of such a fate had his stomach in an uproar.

Through a blur, Brodie surveyed his friends and family. Angel was curled up in one corner, fast asleep, her thumb in her mouth. Buster had undone his tie and was busily working on his shoes. The minister had taken a seat and was leafing through the Bible. The ranch hands focused industriously on the carpet.

Obviously his face gave him away, for the crowd immediately broke into a speculative hum the minute they saw him. Just as Brodie opened his mouth to tell everyone to go home, the front door swung inward and Matilda Jennings burst across the threshold, her iron gray hair in wild disarray, a sheaf of papers clutched in her hand.

"Stop the wedding!" his former housekeeper shouted. "I have proof the bride's a fraud!"

Deannie rode like hellhounds were snarling at her heels.

Ranger galloped across the rough terrain, his hooves skimming over rocks and cactus and tumbleweed. Deannie crouched low in the saddle, her train billowing behind her, pristine as a sail.

It's over.

The tenderness, the compassion, the understanding that had begun as a ruse but quickly turned to love, was lost to her forever. She had deceived Brodie Trueblood in the worst way possible. Then, because she was a coward, as surely as her father had been when he'd faced Rafe Trueblood that awful night so long ago, she'd compounded her sins by allowing him to plan a wedding.

By leaving Brodie at the altar, Deannie had humiliated him in front of his friends and family. How much kinder it would have been to refuse him on the Fourth of July when he'd proposed, instead of letting herself float along on the euphoria of the moment.

She had told herself that everything would be all right. That their love could conquer anything. Anything except promising to marry him under false pretenses.

Brodie deserved someone who would love him freely, unconditionally, with no ulterior motives. For, deep inside her soul, Deannie couldn't say for sure if she'd fallen in love with Brodie the man, or Brodie Trueblood, owner of Willow Creek Ranch.

A hundred different kinds of misery washed over her in unrelenting waves. Deannie swallowed back salty tears. Her nose was stuffed up, and she knew her eyes were red and puffy from crying and riding into the arid wind.

She hadn't consciously headed for the log cabin, but her heart was drawn there, magnetized by the past. Some part of her was still looking for answers, still hoping to discover who in the heck Deanna Rene Hollis, alias Deannie McCellan, really was.

Ranger was breathing hard as he slowed to a trot and scaled the creek bed. Twilight shadows pushed the sun from the sky, and it was almost pitch-black by the time Deannie wheeled the horse into the yard.

Confused and hurting, she tumbled down off the gelding's back and headed for the small sanctuary. Here, she could rest and take a good look at her life. Since her thirst for revenge had evaporated and she would never own Willow Creek, she needed to find a new purpose for being. Preferably an unselfish purpose that would make up for grievous errors.

Fumbling with the knob, Deannie finally ripped the door open and staggered inside, her vision blinded by tears. She flicked on the lights and, blinking, glanced around the room.

It was a far cry from the disheveled mess that had greeted her the day she and Brodie had cleaned the cabin together.

The memory of that day, not so very long ago, snared in her imagination and refused to leave.

She could see him as vividly as if he were standing before her now, looking sumptuous in those fire-engine red bikini briefs. The contours of his well-proportioned fanny coaxing her, the outline of his broad shoulders enticing her, his rugged outdoorsy scent wrapping around her senses and refusing to let go.

"Brodie." Deannie gulped and closed her eyes, willing the erotic vision to dissipate. How long before she forgot the taste of his mouth, the feel of his skin, the sound of his voice, low, deep and tender?

Opening her eyes, she listlessly wandered through the house, taking in the changes. The bedrooms were immaculately clean and neatly organized. Odds and ends had been stored in boxes and their contents clearly labeled. Books. Material. Christmas decorations. Dishes. Linens. Mama's personal things. Rafe's papers.

Deannie's fingers lingered over that box and she sucked in her breath, surprised to find herself shaking at the thought of thumbing through the personal papers of her arch nemesis.

Not really knowing why, she lifted the box from the stack and carried it over to the bed. Pushing her bridal veil from her face, she settled down on the covers and removed the box lid.

The contents smelled of cigar smoke and whiskey. Deannie crinkled her nose, and a sudden jolt of sadness knifed through her. She and Brodie had so much in common. Both with fathers who'd taken the wrong paths in life, both afraid to trust, to let down their guards, both seeking security and stability in the land that meant so much to them.

Deannie leafed through the papers. Doctor bills, bank statements, a lavender-scented birthday card signed "All my love, Melinda.'' She kept digging, not really sure why she was looking.

A final notice from a collection agency postmarked the year Rafe had won the ranch from Gil, a faded photograph of Willow Creek taken from the road and a letter addressed to her father but never mailed.

Deannie's hands trembled so furiously she dropped the letter and it sailed to the floor. Bending over, she reclaimed it and ripped open the sealed envelope. It was dated three weeks before her father had killed himself.

Dear Gil,

I got a confession to make. I ain't proud of what I done, but I done it for a good reason. I don't know if you'll understand and I'm damned sure you won't forgive me, but I got to clear my conscience and tell you what's on my mind. I'm dying and I want to set the record straight. Remember that night you lost Willow Creek? Hell, what am I saying? How could you forget losing your home? Well, truth is, I cheated. I pulled that ace of spades out of my sleeve. I was desperate, and desperate men do desperate things. See, I was about to go to jail for writing hot checks to feed my family. The judge told me if I could prove I had a permanent residence and gainful employment, then he'd give me probation. Plus, Melinda was fixing to leave. She'd finally had enough of living in shacks and puttin' up with my bad habits. I know it's no excuse. I put you and your girl on the street to cover my own tail. I'm sorry for it now and wish to hell I hadn't done it, but I did. I got some money and I'd like to send you a little. It won't make up for nothing, but maybe your girl can use it to go to college or something.

The letter was signed simply, Rafe Trueblood. Enclosed was an offer to send twenty-five thousand dollars.

Deannie stared at the letter as the words sank in. In the last months of his life Rafe Trueblood had been seeking forgiveness. And yet he hadn't mailed the letter. Why not? Had he heard about her father's suicide and decided his debt was eradicated?

A well-worn deck of playing cards with a rubber band wrapped around it lay at the bottom of the box and Deannie just *knew* these were the cards Rafe had used to steal Willow Creek from her father.

In that instant, all her old anger came rushing back. It oozed through her, hot and vicious, as she tasted raw bitterness. She picked up the cards and hurled them against the wall. That felt so good, she tore the letter into tiny pieces and threw it into the air.

Panting, she kicked at the bed and howled her rage. She howled for her missing childhood, for the home she'd forfeited, for the father who'd slipped away from her forever.

But most of all, she howled over losing Brodie.

Deannie gritted her teeth in agony and twisted the skirt of her wedding gown in her fists; she heard the material rip but she no longer cared.

How dare Rafe Trueblood steal everything from her! If he hadn't already been dead, she could have strangled him with her bare hands in that black moment. How many lives had that awful man destroyed? His wife's, her father's, Brodie's. Her own.

"Rafe Trueblood, you lying, conniving, thieving, cheating, son of a…" she swore.

Her chest heaved. Her breath whistled in through her teeth. Her body shuddered. Hatred, that comfortable old emotion, boiled up inside Deannie, embracing her like a friend.

No! A part of her shouted. The part of her that over the

past few months had learned to let go of hatred and replace it with love refused to go unheard.

Then just as quickly as it came, her ire disappeared, dissipating in the aftermath of her adrenaline surge. What was the point? Getting mad would change nothing. Seeking revenge had only made things worse. For the first time in fifteen years, Deanna Rene Hollis saw the past with clear, unbiased eyes.

All this time wasted in holding a grudge. Yes, she'd endured a great injustice. Yes, life wasn't fair. Yes, she'd suffered. But retaliation solved nothing. It only lowered her to Rafe's level. Did she want to end up like the gambler, old and sick, alienated from his family, ostracized by his community, reaching out in the last days of his life with no one to heed his pathetic pleas for forgiveness?

Even if Rafe had cheated, her father had been as much to blame. No one had forced him to drink, no one had held a gun to his head and told him to gamble his homestead on the turn of one card game.

All these years she'd been seeking a monster to hold liable for her woes. Rafe Trueblood had not been a good person, but he was only human. Sure, his motives were shady, but the man had his reasons for his behavior. Beneath that bravado, hidden by booze and a glib attitude, had lurked a sad and lonely man who'd been unable to live up to his responsibilities.

Holding on to hate would not bring her father back. It would not erase the pain she had suffered, nor would it absolve her of the hurt she'd caused Brodie. She'd been wrong to hold him accountable for his father's actions. He was no more answerable for Rafe then she'd been for Gil.

Even if it took a supreme effort of will, she would forgive Rafe Trueblood for what he had done those many years ago, all the while hoping and praying that someday Brodie could find it in his heart to forgive her for lying to him and leaving him standing alone at the altar. It was the only notion that gave Deannie any comfort.

Chapter Eleven

"**Y**our wife-to-be," Matilda said with a malicious cackle, "is none other than the daughter of Gilbert Hollis, the man your father cheated out of Willow Creek."

A collective gasp went up from the crowd. Brodie frowned, absorbing the implication of the woman's words.

Cooter Gates rose to his feet, his eyes stared unseeingly. "Little Deannie's come home?" he whispered. "I thought her voice sounded familiar, but I figured my old ears were playing tricks on me!"

"You bet!" Matilda gleefully shook the paper under Brodie's nose. "This is a copy of her birth certificate and driver's license. Her real name is Deanna Rene Hollis, and I suspect she's marrying you simply to get her hands on this ranch."

"You're wrong," Brodie said harshly to the ex-housekeeper, his voice cracking like a whip. "Deannie just stood me up at the altar, so obviously your supposition is incorrect." He opened his arms wide and made shooing motions. "Show's over folks. Everyone can go home."

With that, he turned on his heels and stalked out of the

house, his mind struggling to process Matilda's jarring revelation.

Deannie was the daughter of Gil Hollis, previous owner of Willow Creek Ranch? The man his father had swindled?

Brodie's ego deflated like a tire going flat. His greatest fear had come to pass. He'd allowed himself to fall in love, only to discover Deannie had faked her affection for him. She'd come back to Willow Creek to reclaim her heritage. That was it. She didn't love him. She never had. It had all been a charade—her kisses, her spontaneous hugs, her sweet declarations of love, a well-orchestrated act and nothing more.

Wincing, Brodie rubbed his throbbing temple. Suddenly everything made perfect sense. Deannie had been at the Lonesome Dove gambling with Kenny in hopes of winning back the ranch the same way her daddy had lost it. Apparently, in the course of the poker game, she'd discovered Brodie had inherited Willow Creek, not his older brother.

A dizzy sensation rocked his head. Brodie could visualize Deannie making her decision to come after him. Finding out he wasn't a gambling man had probably put a temporary kink in her plans. But Deannie was cunning. She was resourceful. She zeroed in on his weakness. She'd taken advantage of his need for love, his desire for a family, and she'd schemed her way into his heart.

She must have faked car problems to weasel her way into Willow Creek. Then Lady Luck had been in her corner when he'd been forced to fire Matilda. He'd been so easy to manipulate. Putty in the hands of a true professional.

He swallowed against the memory. He'd played right into her wily plot, practically begging her to help him with the kids until Patsy Ann returned home from the hospital. And she'd wasted no time making herself indispensable.

Deannie was some kind of actress, he had to give her credit. When she had kissed him, he'd experienced sparks beyond his imagination. The thought that she had simulated her enthusiastic response made his blood run cold. The woman was more heartless and underhanded than Rafe had ever been.

"Damn you, Deannie McCellan!"

Wadding his hands into fists, Brodie rode the wave of betrayal washing through him. Like a helpless buoy on storm-crazed seas, his emotions lashed at him, hard and relentless.

Dunce. Dupe. Sucker.

In his desperate search for love, he'd brought this sorrow upon his own head. He should have checked Deannie's background before hiring her as his housekeeper. He should have asked questions when Rory had discovered nothing amiss with her car. He should have listened to that niggling voice in the back of his mind that urged him not to get involved with a gambling bar dolly.

Instead, he'd been a fool for love. Just like his mother had before him, letting his heart rule his head. Caring about someone who didn't have the capacity or inclination to love him in return.

Guests filtered from the house behind him, talking in hushed tones, but Brodie's personal agony was so great he didn't even notice as they climbed into their vehicles and drove away.

Clutching the corral fence in both hands, he stared across the pasture at the craggy landscape that meant so much to him. The sun was slipping low beyond the horizon, orange and purple fingers of light reaching for one last grasp before nightfall. He studied the tall yellow grass, the short mesquite trees, the mass of cactus. It wasn't the prettiest place in the world, but it was the only home he'd ever known. It was also the land that Deannie McCellan had wanted so badly to possess that she'd been willing to marry a man she did not love in order to obtain it.

But she hadn't gone through with the hoax. At the last minute Deannie had been unable to execute her scheme.

Why?

Had she found the idea of spending the rest of her life hitched to his side completely repugnant? Had the notion been so distasteful that she would even sacrifice Willow Creek to rid herself of him?

Brodie frowned. That theory made no sense. Deannie had already invested so much time and effort in convincing him that she loved him, why would she suddenly shrink back at the thought of lying before the preacher and their friends and family?

Could there be another reason? Could it be that she did indeed love him and therefore couldn't say "I do" under false pretenses? A glimmer of hope flared in his chest, but Brodie didn't dare fan that faint ember.

"Brodie!"

Kenny's shout brought his head up. Brodie turned to see his brother striding toward him.

"Ranger's back."

Brodie's eyes met Kenny's. "And Deannie?"

His brother shook his head. "No sign of her, but Ranger was dragging the saddle behind him."

Anxiety coiled through Brodie's gut. "You think she fell off?"

Kenny shrugged. "Is she a good rider?"

"I don't know," Brodie replied. There were so many things he didn't know about her. He'd assumed his love for her was enough, that it could conquer anything. He'd been so wrong.

"You going to look for her?"

Brodie nodded grimly. He had no choice. It didn't matter whether she loved him or not. He loved her, cared about her, didn't want anything bad to happen to her. He couldn't leave her out there alone in the dark not knowing if she was hurt or scared or lonely. His gut torqued at the thought she could be injured. When he got down to it, her safety meant much more than his own personal anguish.

"Will you put Ranger up for me, Kenny? I'll take the truck and cruise the perimeter."

"Okay." His brother stepped closer. "For what it's worth I hope you and Deannie work things out. If anybody was ever made for each other, you two are."

Shrugging off his brother's comment, Brodie headed for the pickup with Just Married in shoe polish on the windows. Still wearing his tuxedo jacket and black denims, he climbed inside the cab and roared from the driveway, tin cans clanking noisily from the bumper.

The sound mocked him, reminding him of what he'd lost this day. With the heel of one palm, Brodie pushed his hair off his forehead and stared grimly through the marred windshield. He flicked on the headlights, his gaze glued to the swath that sliced through the darkness.

Please let her be all right, he prayed. What would he do if he found her? Brodie clenched his jaw as a worse thought assailed him. What if he didn't find her? She'd be gone and he'd never know for sure the reason that had compelled her to jump from the second-story window and leave him standing at the altar like a fool.

He trod on the accelerator and followed the fence row, his stomach bumping and grinding along with the gearshift.

Without even giving it conscious thought, he turned the truck in the direction of the cabin. Conflicting thoughts ping-ponged in his head, volleying back and forth as he mentally reviewed everything that had happened.

Deannie loves me, she loves me not. His mind vacillated between those two drastic alternatives.

Ten minutes later the pickup crested the rise, and Brodie stared down into the valley where the log cabin crouched beside the creek bed, flanked on either side by an abundance of willow trees.

A lone light shone from the small house, and his heart took wings.

Deannie. It had to be her.

He stopped the truck and killed the engine. He didn't want to pull into the driveway and spook her into running. He had to see her, had to speak to her, had to wring an explanation from her lips.

Shutting the pickup's door quietly, he walked the few yards to the house, his pulse pounding louder, more insistently with each encroaching step.

He hesitated on the front porch, his gaze riveted by what he saw through the window.

Deannie sat on the sofa, an old photograph album in her lap. She still wore her Western-cut wedding gown. The one they'd special-ordered from Dallas.

A lump dominated his throat as he watched her press a tissue to her eyes. She was crying. Over losing Willow Creek? Or could she possibly be crying for him? He didn't want to raise his expectations. Brodie knew he was begging for more heartbreak, but he couldn't seem to quell the hope bubbling in his chest. He had to know for sure.

Galvanized into action, he placed his hand on the knob and wrenched open the door.

Deannie gasped and leaped to her feet, the photo album smacking against the hardwood floor. It fluttered open to a page from the past. Gil Hollis was in the photograph, along with a smiling woman and a small girl on a pony. That red-haired, freckle-faced child had to be Deannie.

She must have unearthed the album from the junk piles stacked high in the bedroom. In that instant Brodie understood her motives. She'd dreamed her whole life of recapturing what she'd lost fifteen years ago. Years lost to her forever. Years destroyed by his father. Years filled with pain and misery and loneliness. Rafe had been to blame for Deannie's sorrow, and no matter how he might wish it, there was no way Brodie could repair the damage.

Raising a trembling hand encased in white kid gloves, Deannie stared at him. "Brodie," she croaked, a myriad of fearful sensations slapping her hard and fast. "Wh-what are you doing here?"

"I might ask you the same question."

His black eyes narrowed to dark accusing slits, his brows knotted over the bridge of his nose. Deannie's heart fluttered helpless as a trapped butterfly beating its wings against a jelly jar.

How handsome he was! Dressed in his wedding apparel, his hair combed off his forehead, his hips cocked forward in that don't-mess-with-me pose, Brodie Trueblood was the most magnificent man she'd ever seen, and Deannie had been inches from becoming his wife.

"Are you all right?" he asked, surprising her with his concern.

She nodded, unable to speak for the emotions sticking to the roof of her mouth like peanut butter.

"You didn't twist your ankle or sprain your arm?"

She shook her head.

"You took quite a jump from that second-story window."

"I landed on my feet," she managed to say at last, still captured by his gaze and feeling very claustrophobic.

"Why did you leave me, Deannie?" he asked quietly. "Why did you make me stand up there all alone, waiting and waiting for you?"

"I never meant to hurt you," she whimpered.

"Don't lie to me." He walked across the floor until they were face-to-face and Deannie could feel his hot, angry breath on her cheek. "I know who you are, Deanna Rene Hollis."

A gasp echoed in the room. Strange, she didn't think the noise came from her lips, but it must have.

"H-h-how long have you known?" she stuttered.

"Matilda Jennings just informed me."

Her knees wobbled, and Deannie feared they'd buckle

beneath her if she remained standing. "I need to sit down," she said.

"I'm sure you do." His tone was cold, sarcastic. His attitude told her she'd wounded him more than words could express.

Placing her hand on the back of the sofa, she eased herself down and took a deep breath. When she'd fled the ranch house, she'd assumed she would never have to face Brodie again. Now that he was here, glaring at her as if she were the worst of sinners, Deannie realized just how badly she'd treated him. She deserved every ounce of his scorn.

"You planned to marry me to get your hands on Willow Creek." He paced the floorboards before her, the ancient wood groaning and creaking beneath his weight.

She couldn't deny it. "Yes. But that was before I knew you."

Brodie gritted his teeth, and an expression of pure anguish rolled over his face. "You should have told me the truth, it wouldn't have changed the way I felt about you."

"Excuse me, but you had enough trouble dealing with the fact I was a gambler. You think you would have given me the job as your housekeeper if you'd known I was Gil Hollis's daughter?"

"Does the word *trust* mean anything to you?" His nostrils flared.

"Trust a Trueblood? You've got to be joking. My father trusted your father to play a fair poker game and Rafe cheated. I found a letter he wrote to my father confessing the whole thing. Rafe knew what he was doing. He understood the repercussions—that a seven-year-old child would end up on the streets. The hell of it was, he didn't care."

"I'm not my father, Deannie, and you should know that by now. I'm sorry for what he did to your father. It hurts me in innumerable ways, but I can't undo the past."

"I do know that," she said miserably. "That's why I

couldn't go through with the wedding. I couldn't make you pay for your father's sins, although heaven knows I wanted to.''

Brodie's jaw clenched. The expression in his eyes was cold and forgiving.

He had every right to hate her. She'd done nothing but lie to him from the very start. She'd attempted to cheat him just as Rafe had cheated Gil, and she'd caused Brodie unthinkable pain.

How she wanted to reach out to him, to touch that dear face, to fall on her knees and beg his forgiveness.

"There's just one thing I need to know," he said, his voice cracking with emotion.

"Yes?" She clasped her hands together in her lap. They curled like doves fallen by a hunter's gun—still, lifeless, dead.

"I want the truth." He swung his hard gaze, knife-blade sharp, at her.

Silently, she nodded.

"You never really loved me, did you? It was a pretext. Come on, tell me how you planned it, how you lay awake at night thinking of ways to deceive me. Tell me how you secretly laughed at my gullibility behind my back."

"Brodie." Deannie rose to her feet and started toward him, her hand extended in a gesture of peace and regret. "It wasn't like that."

"Don't," he said, twisting away from her, "even think about touching me."

His rejection hurt worse than a million physical blows, but she had earned every bit of his disdain and more.

"I'm so sorry," she whispered, tears streaming down her cheeks. "I tried to leave before you asked me to marry you. On the Fourth of July, remember?"

Brodie nodded. "So why didn't you tell me the truth then?"

Deannie's bottom lip trembled. "I couldn't bear to go, not after you proposed."

"Because of Willow Creek?" The look in his brown eyes was one of hollow defeat.

"Because of you."

He rubbed a hand along his jaw. "You don't know how much I'd like to believe that."

"I swear it's the truth. I'm not going to deny that for the past fifteen years I've been waiting for the chance to seek revenge upon Rafe Trueblood for what he did to me and my daddy. I lived for the day I could confront him face-to-face. In my mind, all I could think about was getting my home back. I didn't even remember Rafe had two sons until I met Kenny at the Lonesome Dove."

Brodie ran his hands through his hair. "I guess that's when you discovered I had inherited the ranch and not my brother."

Deannie nodded.

"That's when you realized you couldn't gamble the ranch away from me."

"Yes."

"So you decided to marry me."

"That pretty well sums it up."

"And yet you expect me to believe that somewhere along the line you really fell in love with me?" Brodie paced the short span of the living room, his hands clasped behind his back. The sight yanked on her emotions. She hated the turmoil she'd caused him.

"That's exactly what happened," she whispered.

"Listen, I apologize for my father and what he did. His actions were reprehensible, but that does not excuse your behavior."

Deannie swallowed. "I know that now. My lust for revenge has destroyed any chance for us, hasn't it?"

Her heart ached unlike any agony she'd ever experienced before. It was far worse even than the hurt she'd experienced on that awful night Rafe had escorted her and her father off Willow Creek. That had been beyond her control, but this disaster was of her own making.

Brodie shook his head. "It took so much for me to finally trust you. I was so afraid to love, so terrified I'd end up like my mother, caring about someone who couldn't love me back." His laugh was an ugly cackle without a trace of mirth. "Despite my best intentions, despite the care I took, I fell right into the same trap."

"But, Brodie," Deannie whimpered. "I do love you. With all my heart and soul. That's why I ran from the wedding. I couldn't marry you under false pretenses."

"Lord, Deannie, how I'd like to believe you." He looked at her, and his eyes were red-rimmed and close to tears.

"I'm so sorry, Brodie. There's nothing I can do to change what I've done, but I'm begging you to give me a second chance. Please? Could we try again? And this time there'll be no more secrets and no thoughts of revenge keeping us from truly getting to know each other."

Brodie's gaze swept her trembling body. He couldn't renounce the yearning inside him. He wanted her, no matter what her faults. She'd laid everything on the line, confessed her failings. Now it was his turn, for he wasn't without culpability.

All this time, he'd been afraid to give himself completely to her. He'd held his emotions in reserve, ready to pull them back if she showed signs of not living up to his ideal. He'd uselessly been trying to protect himself. If he loved, then he loved. And he'd loved Deannie McCellan from the moment she'd stepped into the headlights of his pickup truck.

Urged on by the feelings sweeping through his body like a hurricane, Brodie trod heavily across the floor toward her. Without another word, he gathered her into his arms and planted his fiery brand upon her waiting mouth.

Lord, had anyone ever tasted so sweet? All his suffering disappeared in her embrace. Her arms went around his neck. Her grateful fingers entangled in his hair. Her quiet noises of pleasure stoked his emotions to a fever pitch.

"Look me in the eyes, Deanna Rene Hollis," Brodie said, breaking his lips from hers and cupping her petite chin in his palm.

She gulped but held his gaze.

"Do you want to come home to Willow Creek?"

"Not if it means hurting you. I'd rather leave forever than have you doubt my love."

"Shhh," he placed one finger over her lips. "Answer my questions. Do you want to assume your rightful place as mistress of Willow Creek? Do you want to be my wife and live on this land for the rest of your life? Do you want to have our children here and watch them grow? Do you want to mend the hurt our fathers caused so long ago?"

"Oh, Brodie," Deannie sighed, happiness beyond words flooding her body. She'd dreamed of this moment for fifteen years. Coming home. Finding a man to love. A man as good and kind and strong as Brodie Trueblood. At last that moment had arrived, and all her suffering came to an end in his loving embrace. "I do, I do, I do."

*   *   *   *   *

DIANA PALMER
ANN MAJOR
SUSAN MALLERY

RETURN TO WHITEHORN

In **April 1998** get ready to catch the bouquet. Join in the excitement as these bestselling authors lead us down the aisle with three heartwarming tales of love and matrimony in Big Sky country.

A very engaged lady is having second thoughts about her intended; a pregnant librarian is wooed by the town bad boy; a cowgirl meets up with her first love. Which Maverick will be the next one to get hitched?

Available in **April 1998.**

Silhouette's beloved **MONTANA MAVERICKS** returns in Special Edition and Harlequin Historicals starting in February 1998, with brand-new stories from your favorite authors.

Round up these great new stories at your favorite retail outlet.

Take 4 bestselling love stories FREE

a FREE surprise gift!

Special Limited-time Offer

Mail to Silhouette Reader Service™

3010 Walden Avenue
P.O. Box 1867
Buffalo, N.Y. 14240-1867

YES! Please send me 4 free Silhouette Romance™ novels and my free surprise gift. Then send me 6 brand-new novels every month, which I will receive months before they appear in bookstores. Bill me at the low price of $2.90 each plus 25¢ delivery and applicable sales tax, if any.* That's the complete price and a savings of over 10% off the cover prices—quite a bargain! I understand that accepting the books and gift places me under no obligation ever to buy any books. I can always return a shipment and cancel at any time. Even if I never buy another book from Silhouette, the 4 free books and the surprise gift are mine to keep forever.

215 SEN CF2P

Name	(PLEASE PRINT)	
Address	Apt. No.	
City	State	Zip

ALICIA SCOTT

**Continues the
twelve-book series—
36 Hours—in March 1998
with Book Nine**

PARTNERS IN CRIME

The storm was over, and Detective Jack Stryker finally had a
prime suspect in Grand Springs' high-profile murder case. But
beautiful Josie Reynolds wasn't about to admit to the crime—
nor did Jack want her to. He believed in her innocence, and he
teamed up with the alluring suspect to prove it. But was he
playing it by the book—or merely blinded by love?

For Jack and Josie and *all* the residents of Grand Springs,
Colorado, the storm-induced blackout was just the beginning of
36 Hours that changed *everything!* You won't want to miss a
single book.

Available at your favorite retail outlet.

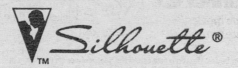

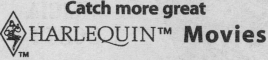 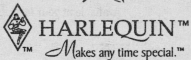

THE BABY OF THE MONTH CLUB

RITA
-Award-
Winning
Author

MARIE FERRARELLA's

*miniseries continues with her
brand-new Silhouette single title*

In The Family Way

Dr. Rafe Saldana was Bedford's most popular pediatrician. And though the handsome doctor had a whole lot of love for his tiny patients, his heart wasn't open for business with women. At least, not until single mother Dana Morrow walked into his life. But Dana was about to become the newest member of the Baby of the Month Club. Was the dashing doctor ready to play daddy to her baby-to-be?

Available June 1998.

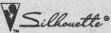

Silhouette®

Find this new title by Marie Ferrarella
at your favorite retail outlet.

Return to the Towers!

In March
New York Times bestselling author

NORA ROBERTS

brings us to the Calhouns' fabulous
Maine coast mansion and reveals the
tragic secrets hidden there for generations.

For all his degrees, Professor Max Quartermain has a
lot to learn about love—and luscious Lilah Calhoun is
just the woman to teach him. Ex-cop Holt Bradford is
as prickly as a thornbush—until Suzanna Calhoun's
special touch makes love blossom in his heart.
And all of them are caught in the race to solve
the generations-old mystery of a priceless
lost necklace…and a timeless love.

Lilah and Suzanna
THE
Calhoun Women

A special 2-in-1 edition containing
FOR THE LOVE OF LILAH and
SUZANNA'S SURRENDER

Available at your favorite retail outlet.